BLUE BLOODS

&

BLACK HEARTS

A Larry Gillam and Sam Lovett Novel

by

WILLIAM N. GILMORE

William N. Gilmore

First printing

Book cover design by William N. Gilmore and by Arewa Lanre of graphics_pro360 (a Fiverr.com seller)

This is a work of fiction. Names, characters, places, and incidents are the product of the author's imagination or are used fictitiously, and any resemblance to actual persons, living or dead, businesses, companies, events, or locals are entirely coincidental.

ISBN:9780692810019

Manufactured by createspace

www.createspace.com

Printed in the United States of America

BLUE BLOODS

&

BLACK HEARTS

Merry Christmas.
Grand Pa

William N. Gilmore
APD

WILLIAM N. GILMORE

William N. Gilmore

Acknowledgements

I've had a lot of help and encouragement from many people on this work. It's taken me a while to write and even longer to put into this form. I hope you enjoy it, if not, they are to blame.

Thanks to these wonderful people

My wife Esther, our family, and many friends.

Deanna Oaks, Bryan Powell, the late Dana Freeman, and the rest of the Paulding County (GA) Writers Guild.
pcwg-ga@pcwgga.org.

I dedicate this work to all my brothers and sisters in law enforcement and to their families; hoping you will be together after every shift of every day. And to our heroes who made the ultimate sacrifice, we will forever remember and honor you, and your stars will forever shine.

Remembering my friend and colleague; the brightest star of them all:

Detective Sherry Lyons-Williams

Atlanta Police Department

End of Watch - April 4th, 2001

William N. Gilmore

CHAPTER 1

Jessie is young, rather tall for her age, and thin as a rail. There are two things not obviously apparent about Jessie; the first being that she is a prostitute, and the other, which even she is unaware, is that she only has a short time to live.

She just finished with her latest trick, an elderly white guy who paid her twenty-five dollars for her special services. She then walked the short distance to the local convenience store, owned by an elderly Asian couple, to buy herself a beer and a pack of cigarettes.

She used a fake ID she bought downtown; one with an earlier birth date than her real one; not that she needed it there, the old store owners turned a blind eye to what went on in the neighborhood and catered to all the young drug dealers and other lowlifes not just to bolster their sales, but to keep from having trouble.

Jessie also purchased a shooter pack for an extra two dollars. The shooter pack was a small, pre-packaged paper bag containing a four-inch glass tube with a small artificial flower in it; a small piece of copper scouring pad, and a book of matches. This was all she needed to replace the used-up crack pipe she broke earlier.

She continued her mission to an old clapboard house just down the street; a place she visited many times, it was well known in the neighborhood. Along the way, she finished the beer and tossed the can into the street, knowing some wino would pick it up later for the aluminum. The recycling price per pound kept going up over the months.

Arriving at the dilapidated house, she went onto the old wooden porch and up to the big metal burglar door. It was nothing more than an iron frame with one-inch bars from top to bottom about four inches apart. It was covered with a mesh screen which was torn in many places, and a hole near the scratched-up brass lock, big enough to put your hand through. Before Jessie could knock on it, a big mountain of a guy came to the door; more fat than muscle, and lots of it.

"What you want?" he asked, in a deep, gruff voice.

"Gimme a dime," Jessie said to the man as she slid a ten-dollar bill through the hole in the screen. The man took the money, disappeared for about ten seconds, returning with a tiny zip-locked plastic bag. The opening was melted shut, and it contained a small, off-white chunk of crack cocaine. He pushed it through the screen and into her waiting hand.

"Hey man," she said, looking at the bag, "this ain't no dime. You know me. I ain't one of them white fools that drives up here from College Park. You need to gimme better than this."

The big dealer just looked at Jessie for a few seconds and said, "Okay, give me ten more and I'll give you two more sacks."

Jessie thought about this for a second, then reached into the pocket of her dirty jeans and removed ten more dollars and stuck it through the hole in the screen. The dealer took the money, left again, and returned shortly with two additional sacks handing them to Jessie. She put the sacks into her pocket and walked away from the house and back towards the grocery store feeling she negotiated a good deal. She even skipped a bit.

When Jessie got back to the store, she went behind the building where she would be out of sight of the public, but more importantly, out of sight of the police if they were to drive by. She retrieved the shooter pack out of her back pocket, sat down on an old, red plastic Coke crate, and popped open the stapled paper bag, removing the contents.

She removed the fake tulip from the tube, tossing it away; sometimes, it would be a rose. She tore off a small part of the bright copper pad, jamming it into one end of the four-inch long, glass pipe using the old piece of wire hanger she always kept with her, leaving it just about a quarter-inch from the end.

Next, she reached into her pocket removing a small, one-inch piece of rubber tubing she kept from her old, broken pipe which she put on the opposite end of the new glass pipe to keep it from burning her lips. She took out one of the sacks of dope she just bought, tore open the bag and placed the small rock of

9

crack cocaine into the pipe against the copper.

Jessie used her own cigarette lighter to light the crack; she didn't like using matches, they were too quick and unreliable. Jessie put the pipe in her mouth and held the lighter under the end with the crack. The heat slowly melted the rock of cocaine and Jessie sucked the fumes deep into her lungs. As she held the cigarette lighter to the crack, she continued to inhale.

It didn't take long until she began to feel the effects of the cocaine. However, it was never like the first time she used it, almost three years ago, when she was fifteen. Moreover, it seemed to take longer and more dope each time to get high. She would never relive the first-time experience of the euphoric feeling the drug gave, nonetheless, she would never give up trying either.

Jessie decided to take out one of the two remaining sacks and smoked that one too. She figured she would find one of the junkies or winos hanging in the area, or maybe even one of her tricks to buy the last sack for ten dollars. She could make some of her money back. If not, she would just save it for later.

She sat there for a while after finishing the second rock and enjoyed the short-lived high the crack was giving her. The highs didn't last more than ten to fifteen minutes these days, and she was thinking about smoking the last rock when she noticed things around her began to look more and more out of focus.

She shook her head, however, the fog remained. Soon, she began having difficulty breathing and was having a hard time keeping her balance on the plastic box. Jessie felt a trickle under her nose and wiped at it with the back of her hand. When she pulled it away, she saw her hand was smeared with blood.

There was fire in her stomach, bowels, and bladder as if some creature inside was clawing its way out. Her head felt like it might split in two or just explode altogether. The strange effects of smoking the crack came on like a volcano suddenly erupting.

"Damn!" she wheezed. A hit of crack never did that to her before. She tried to stand, but her legs wobbled and would not cooperate as she slid hard off the crate.

As Jessie lay there, she tried to form the words to yell for help, but her mind was now almost too far gone and all that came out of her mouth was a gurgling sound and red foam bubbles of blood. With her last conscience thought, Jessie wondered if maybe she shouldn't have smoked the second hit of crack.

ᖇ

"Yeow! Damn it, Gillam!" Sam swore. "Why don't you watch what you're doing?"

Detective Sergeant Larry Gillam pulled the unmarked detective car away from the fast food's drive-through window with a quick burst of speed just as his partner, Sam Lovett, was adding the contents of the small, non-dairy creamer packet to his drink, spilling some of the hot, steaming coffee onto Sam's lap.

"I was," answered Gillam. "I just wasn't watching what you were doing. Sorry about that."

"Now I'll have to change when we get back to the office. You know, I don't like you very much right now."

"Yeah, I know, but I sure am glad you love me." Gillam batted his eyes at Lovett.

"Love this," Lovett replied, as he dabbed at his wet and stained pants with a napkin.

"No thanks," Larry said, laughing. "You know I don't like coffee."

Gillam and Lovett had been partners in the Narcotics Squad for four years. Gillam, having been there for seven, teamed with several partners, but none like Lovett.

Gillam was a veteran of the Atlanta Police Department, serving for 15 years and distinguished himself with numerous large drug arrests and seizures which kept most of his superiors happy. Gillam liked being a detective; more than being a sergeant. He always referred to himself and preferred being called, 'Detective'. Although he reluctantly took the tests for lieutenant, he did not want the responsibilities which came with the rank. There were too many headaches and lousy days off in the beginning and sometimes for years.

He paid his dues and worked his way to the day shift with weekends off. He loved working dope. To him, there was nothing better than getting dealers off the street and taking away their drugs, guns, and money, along with their fancy cars. Anything he could do to disrupt their operations for a while. Unfortunately, the courts exhibited other ideas.

With the jails overcrowded, the smart-assed, high paid defense attorneys, judges who don't care, and an understaffed, underfunded public defender's office which would just as soon get a rapist off as a drunk and disorderly, it was a wonder anyone got any time, much less convicted.

This profession Gillam loved turned into a dark obsession and he let it take over his life. He ended up spending more and more time at work. Partly the reason for his two divorces. Lucky, to some degree, there were not any children. Now he lives in a two-bedroom apartment with his cat, Cali. More than just a cat, she was his best friend; next to the human, Sam, that is.

He dated very little, but since his last divorce just over a year ago, he was just not ready to try to make a go at another relationship yet. Sam tried to get Larry to go out more with him and his wife and tried setting him up with some of her single friends, but Larry just wasn't one to socialize. Besides Sam and Cali, his best friends were his Smith & Wesson semi-autos and any book or movie dealing with science fiction.

Larry wasn't a bad-looking fellow. He was 5'11", weighed 180 pounds, and still possessed most of his hair and teeth. He just wasn't much of a people person, and he was too much of a loner. If Sam took a day off or was out sick, he would go it alone instead of working with any of the other members of the squad unless they needed him on a raid or to sign reports. Not that he didn't trust them or like them. He just preferred his own company at times.

Sam was almost the opposite. He was only 5'6", thin, and he worked at having a life. He and his wife, Debbie, together now for six wonderful years, were still waiting on kids.

Sam was more outgoing and showed a natural way with people, sometimes having to calm Larry down in certain situations. Sometimes Larry took the job way too serious, almost personal.

Sam genuinely liked Gillam and enjoyed goading him when things were slow. It seemed to help make their relationship work; even if Gillam *was* his superior officer. Moreover, it released some of the stress which comes with this type of job. Always the thought in the back of their heads that today could be their last.

Sam was with the department for five years before being promoted to detective and assigned to Narcotics. He wasn't sure he would enjoy working dope. He would rather have been assigned to either the Homicide or Robbery Squad. Working with Gillam the past four years made things easier. He was a good teacher, experienced in street smarts.

When Lovett first got to the Narcotics Squad, he put in transfers to go to one of the other squads, however, each time he was denied. Sam thought it might have been because of Lieutenant Mark Jones.

Lovett thought Jones kept him in the Narcotics Squad as a punishment because of an incident involving a friend of Jones. While still in the uniform division, Lovett stopped a drunk driver who resisted arrest and took a swing at him. Lovett decked the man to gain control of him. The guy ended up with a broken nose and a ride to jail.

Jones was a sergeant in another area at the time. He got word from his friend and attempted to persuade Lovett to drop the charges. Lovett refused to do it and felt Jones was retaliating against him ever since.

When Jones made lieutenant, and became the commander of the Narcotics Squad just a week after Sam got there, Lovett knew he would have to watch his step around him. Little did he know just how close he was going to have to watch.

William N. Gilmore

CHAPTER 2

A call came over the police radio requesting a Narcotics unit to meet with a Homicide detective behind the Lee Grocery Store on Lowery Boulevard.

Gillam and Lovett answered the call, arriving within fifteen minutes. When they pulled up to the store, they saw several uniform cars and the crime scene van parked out front with a crowd of people all around.

One young officer was putting up the crime scene tape and trying to get people to stay back. He was obviously a rookie. Neither Gillam nor Lovett remember having seen him before, and they noticed his uniform and leather gear were new. However, the real telltale sign was that he was wearing his hat. Veteran uniform officers almost never wore their hats.

As they approached the scene, Gillam showed the officer his badge and the rookie came to attention, identifying himself as Officer Adams.

"I was the one who discovered the body," Adams said, with almost a sound of pride. "I've just been on this beat for a couple of weeks now. I was checking the area for junkies and homeless people, and found the girl behind the store. I've seen her before, but I don't know much about her. Are you guys with Homicide too?"

"No, we're with Narcotics," Lovett stated. "We're not sure what's up yet, nonetheless, we got a call to come by here."

"That's great," Adams beamed. "I hope to get into Narcotics someday. That's what I really want to do."

"Well, keep up the good work and with a little luck you might make it one day," Gillam said, giving the young man some encouragement. "How about showing us who's in charge here."

Adams directed the detectives towards the back of the building. When they turned the corner of the building, they saw a crime scene technician taking photographs of an apparent young woman lying on her side, her back almost against the building, and her face pointed into the blood-soaked ground. There was a foul odor of defecation, urine, and blood emanating from the body.

They walked up to Detective John Starling who was talking with an Asian man; most likely, he was the owner or an employee of the store.

Starling turned towards the detectives. "Thanks for getting here so quickly. How the heck are you, Lovett? Haven't seen you in a while."

Starling stuck his hand out, and Lovett shook it saying, "I'm doing well. You know my partner, Gillam, don't you?"

"We've met," Gillam said, as he shook the other detective's hand. At least he thought they may have at some point and although he didn't know much about Starling, he heard the he was a good Homicide Detective.

"So, tell us, what can we do for you?" Lovett inquired.

"I've got a body over there with blood and body fluids oozing from every orifice, and with no apparent signs of any force," Starling began. "I'm not sure yet how she died, but I think it was from a stroke, possibly drug induced. We're still required to respond to unknown causes of death just in case," he added.

"There was some drug paraphernalia around the body and a rock of suspected crack cocaine in her pocket along with some cash, and an obvious fake identification card," Starling continued as they walked over to the body. "No one around here seems to have seen anything or knows much except that she's a hooker, and her real name was Jessie."

"Jessie!" Lovett blurted out. "That's Jessie? We've known her for years out here. She's a regular. Why, we even locked her up again just last month for prostitution," he said, as he bent down and looked over the body; his hand covering his nose and mouth.

"Yeah, that's right," Gillam added. "I think her last name is Ryder. We caught her in a cemetery with this old fart banging away at her in the bed of a pick-up. Not a pretty sight," Gillam grimaced, "but then again, a lot better than this."

"Yeah," Lovett interjected as he got up and they all moved away from the stench of the body. "I remember that. We didn't even wait till he was through," he laughed. "You could say we scared the pants *on* him."

"Anyway," Starling laughed and continued, "I just wanted someone from your unit to know what's going on. I doubt if it's a robbery attempt or domestic dispute. This may be just a simple case of an overdose; however, I don't ever remember seeing one like this. It seems she got hold of something she couldn't handle, and I thought you guys might have some insight into something like this."

Starling pulled a small, clear, zip-locked bag from a larger evidence bag and handed it to Gillam. "This is what I found in her pocket," he said. "Looks like a rock of crack cocaine to me, but you're the experts."

Gillam held the bag up and inspected the contents. "Looks like you're right. Maybe a dime's worth. More likely a nick," he said, as he handed the bag to his partner. "I wonder how many she smoked."

"I also found this pipe beside her," Starling said, removing it from the evidence bag. "It looks almost new."

"She probably just bought it from the store," Lovett said, as he looked at the glass pipe. "We're going to turn you into a Narcotics Detective yet,"

"No thanks," Starling replied. "You can keep all the ones who argue and fight back. I'll deal mainly with the ones who don't have much to say anymore. I'll go ahead and question the owner of the store some more though. I can put some added pressure on him now about possibly selling drug paraphernalia.

Maybe I'll get some better information as to when she

was in there and get a closer time of death. Possibly even where she may have gotten the crack. I'm going to try to have the Medical Examiner do a rush job for me so hopefully we might know something by this afternoon or early this evening. He owes me."

"Thanks a lot, John," Lovett said, handing Starling back his evidence. "Keep us advised on what you find out. If there's anything more we can do, just give us a call, and if you don't mind, send a copy of the report over to me. I'll see if any of our guys have run into anything similar."

"That I'll do, and thanks a bunch," Starling said, over his shoulder as he began to walk over to the crime scene technician.

"That's a shame about Jessie," Lovett said, as they walked back to their car.

"It sure is," Gillam returned. "I thought she was a lot smarter than that."

"Me too." Lovett agreed. "That cocaine is a powerful demon, and sometimes, the cure seems worse than the disease."

"We've seen it way too many times. The best cure for that disease," Gillam nodded in reply, "is to never start. You're hooked from the very first time."

As the two detectives drove away from the store, the people crowding up against the crime scene tape reminded Gillam of vultures waiting for their next victim.

The second most important part of the day was soon upon

Gillam and Lovett. They needed to decide where they were going to have lunch. Of course, the *most* important part of any day was safely going off duty, which was still several hours away. The new twelve-hour shifts for the Narcotics Squad sucked. The over-time pay was great.

"Well," Lovett said, "what do you feel like today?"

"I'm not sure," Gillam snickered, "why don't you reach over here and feel me and see."

"That was almost funny," smiling at his partner's stupid joke. "But don't you think it's time for you to get some new material?"

"Okay, okay," Gillam laughed. "You used to laugh at that, but I guess it did get old after the first couple hundred times. You pick today. I still owe you five bucks from the Braves game the other day. That is, unless you want to go double or nothing with tonight's game?"

"No, not tonight. They should whip the Philly's butts this time. That new rookie is pitching. He's unbeaten."

"Yeah, let's hope so," Gillam wished. "That guy is awesome. Now if we could just get the bats to heat up we would have another World Series here with no problem."

"Hey," Lovett interjected. "That reminds me; I might be able to get some tickets for one of the games this weekend against the Dodgers if you want to go."

"Sounds good to me. I don't have any pressing appointments I know of. Just let me know which night."

"Okay. I think Deb wants to go and she may bring one of her girlfriends along."

"Oh, now I see," Gillam said, shaking his head. "Another set up. When are you going to get it in your thick head I don't need any help getting a date if I want one?"

"Come on Larry, you haven't gone on a date in how long? Three months, maybe four?"

"Not since you set me up with Ms. Godzilla for dinner over at your place. I was waiting for the Japanese Army to come put out her breath. That alone was enough to level a small city. And she was about the same size as that monster too."

"Okay," Sam chuckled. "So, you didn't find your true love that night. Doesn't mean you give up trying. This friend of Deb's is a real knock out, she's really funny, and she *likes* cops."

"Good! You go out with her."

"Deb's told her a lot about you," Sam prodded. "She's very interested in meeting you."

"If she knows too much, I'll have to kill her," Larry said. "What does she look like, anyway? He tried to ask without sounding too interested. "Is she a dwarf or a bearded lady? Does she have more than two eyes or only one?"

"She's about 5-9 and she has long, red hair, and green eyes; two arms, two legs, two teeth and an IQ of almost two," Sam chuckled. "But really, she's not bad at all. That's about all I know. You can ask Deb if there is any more you want to know. What would it hurt?"

"You know I'm a sucker for red hair."

"You're a sucker for anything female. That's why I have to hide my dog whenever you come over."

"Yeah, it has been a long time. The cat is getting harder to catch."

"You're sick," Lovett said, with mock disgust.

"Maybe that's why we get along so well together," Gillam replied.

"Maybe so, but I still wish you wouldn't give me those deep, longing looks."

"Shut up and let's go feed our faces and get some work done today. I'm sure your favorite lieutenant would appreciate that."

"Screw the sorry sack of Siberian sheep dip!" Lovett exclaimed. "Are you trying to ruin my appetite?"

"Just trying to do my part to keep you in a tip top, lean, mean, fighting machine figure," Gillam replied, laughing.

"Screw you too." Sam said as he took his sunglasses off, wiped them clean with a doughnut shop napkin, and then replaced them.

The noonday sun was glaring down, and the temperature was starting to rise into the mid-nineties, which was close to average for the middle of August. However, things were about to get much hotter for Gillam and Lovett, and it had nothing to do with the Atlanta weather.

CHAPTER 3

The three boys were enjoying the weekday afternoon's warmth, knowing school would start again in another couple of weeks. Their day was filled with baseball, games, hanging out, and just being boys.

Now they were going exploring as most young boys do when there weren't enough of the guys around to play ball or play other games. Sometimes these expeditions proved to be profitable. There were all kinds of things to find; things which could be used in their hidden fort, to work on, or just take apart.

Willie was the oldest at twelve; however, not necessarily the smartest of the group. Once, he found an old television he enjoyed working on until he plugged it in and filled his parent's garage with smoke.

James, Willie's brother, was only a year younger, but seemed more responsible and spent a lot of his time with Willie trying to keep him out of trouble and away from street thugs and gang bangers. This was mostly a full-time job.

The pressure to join the neighborhood gang was strong and the members felt if you weren't a part of the gang, then you were against it. The gangs were into drug dealing, auto thefts, and burglaries and James heard they even were involved in some home invasions and robberies. Most of the gang members spent time in jail or boot camp. A lot of them were just kids themselves.

Curtis was the youngest of the three, but knew too well about gangs. His older brother would have been nineteen this year if a rival gang hadn't shot him down during a drive-by two years ago. Several years before that tragic day, Curtis and his brother went to live with their aunt. It was after their mother decided she wanted to do her own thing and not be tied down. She abandoned them and hasn't been heard from since.

Today, none of the bad stuff was on their minds. It was a day to be young and happy, and it seemed as if they would have the whole world to themselves. The first thing on their list of activities during the expedition was to fix up the fort they built in the wooded area close to their neighborhood.

The fort was their secret place and each swore not to tell anyone about it. It wasn't much, just some old plywood boards between trees covered by a tarp. There was also an old wooden door with the hinges nailed to one tree while a long chain ran through the hole where the doorknob used to be, padlocking it around another tree. They believed it necessary to secure it to keep the street people known as, *urban campers*, out.

They walked a short distance into the woods, and there between several old oak trees, which were used as supports and walls, was their fort; to them it was a magnificent castle.

As they approached the fort, they checked on several booby traps they made to give early warnings of intruders.

Everything appeared in order, and Curtis pulled out his key to unlock the big silver lock which his aunt bought for him. He told her he wanted to use it to lock-up his bike. All three boys possessed their own key for the lock. Curtis, using part of his allowance, made extras for them, or if any became lost.

There was a musty smell inside the fort, and the dirt floor was a little damp. The dirty, blue tarp roof gave it an eerie turquoise hue in the early afternoon sun.

"It's time to make another trip for wood and stuff," Willie said. "We need to build the fort bigger and to be able to make it stand against the weather better, and besides, some of the boards are rotting and starting to stink."

"I thought that was your feet I smelled," James laughed.

Curtis burst out laughing as well. He always laughed at their jokes. More to be a part of the group than thinking they were funny. That one was.

At eight-years old, he felt lucky to have friends like Willie and James. Not everyone wanted a younger kid hanging around with them, but Willie and James were almost like family to him. Ever since his brother was killed, the three were nearly inseparable. Curtis' aunt also felt better knowing there was someone around other than gang bangers.

The boys took out of the fort the old rusty shopping cart, which they used to haul all their found treasures. They maneuvered the cart through the woods to the street, and were able to push the wobbly cart easily enough then.

They decided to head towards some of the abandoned houses a few streets over. There was usually a good supply of wood, but then again, other valued things such as window glass and bricks were so dirty, they wouldn't even think about bringing them back until they were washed. Occasionally, they would even find books or lamps and sometimes, furniture.

As the boys walked along pushing the cart, they laughed at each other's silly jokes. Curtis began trotting backwards and taunted the other two to try to catch him. He turned and ran up the street a few yards. When he saw neither Willie nor James chasing him, he slowed down, and again began taunting them even more to catch him.

"Hey, what's wrong with you guys? Too old to catch me? Don't tell me I'm faster than either of you?" Curtis teased, laughing.

Willie yelled back at Curtis, "We got this buggy to push. Why don't you run on ahead and hide and we'll try to find you. A good game of hide and seek before we get busy. Okay?"

"All right!" Curtis yelled. "You'll never find me. I'll be like the invisible man," he said, as he ran off towards the abandoned houses.

When Curtis was out of hearing range, James said, "We ain't gonna' find him cause we ain't goin' be lookin' for him."

Willie busted out laughing having to hold onto the cart to keep from falling in the street. He thought James pulled a fast one over on Curtis. Little did they know, Curtis was pulling one over on them. It was his plan to run ahead to find the best stuff before they could have a chance to claim anything. He would be the hero of the day.

Curtis ran up to one of the boarded doorways of the dilapidated houses and squeezed through a plywood covering which was pried loose on one side. The house stunk as did most of the abandoned houses in the area. The pungent odors from rotting wood, mildewed carpet, and being used as a bathroom by homeless people and junkies, hung in the lifeless air. The heat made it so much worse.

There was little light filtering through the ill-fitting, board-covered windows and doors and Curtis was having a hard time adjusting to the near dark. He went into one of the other rooms where one of the window coverings was loose, looking like it was about to fall off any minute. The smell here was worse than any other house he had ever been in. He started to walk over to the window when he tripped over something on the floor. Curtis got up, wiping his hands on his pants.

"Oh, crap!" Curtis said. They appeared wet, and he thought maybe he may have fallen where someone used the bathroom. He gingerly smelled his hands and gagged. They didn't have the odor he was expecting. It was worse. A gag factor of at least ten.

Curtis walked over to the covered window and with just a little effort, pushed the loose plywood board off the window with both hands, allowing the mid-afternoon sunlight to come in. He blinked away the bright light until he was able once again to see clearly. He then saw his hands were covered in red.

"Damn," Curtis mumbled, looking at his hands. "I fell in some stupid red paint." He turned and saw the red spot on the floor where he fell and followed it, expecting to see a turned over can of paint. Instead, there was a much larger something on the floor than a can of paint. There on the floor was someone or what may have once been someone with what he believed was blood all around the head.

Curtis stared with his mouth wide open, slowly backing until his back hit a wall. He looked down at his hands, saw the red stains once again as his mind put it together, and began running and screaming back to where he came in.

He got outside and began rubbing his hands frantically in the grass and dirt and was screaming and crying at the same time.

James and Willie heard Curtis before they saw him. They began running towards the house leaving the cart behind in the middle of the street. They saw Curtis rubbing his hands in the grass trying to get what appeared to be blood off his hands and thought he must have cut himself on some glass, a nail, or something, trying to get in. There were also red stains which must have been blood on his pants and his shoes.

Curtis was still screaming and yelling and even though they were right there with him, they couldn't understand him.

Willie grabbed Curtis' hands looking for cuts and James

pulled out his handkerchief and started to wipe Curtis' hands.

Curtis stopped screaming, but was blubbering through his tears and sobs about something in the house.

"What's wrong with you?" James asked, still filled with concern for his friend. "I don't see no cuts on you."

"There's somethin' in there," Curtis finally got out, pointing towards the house. "Somethin' awful. Somethin' dead, and I got it on me." Curtis clutched James' handkerchief, wiping at his hands furiously although almost all of the blood was already off.

"What was it, Curt?" Willie asked, in excitement. "An animal, like a dog, a cat, or somethin'?"

"I bet it was a possum," James countered. "They can get mean sometimes. It didn't bite you, did it? If you get bit by one of them, you got to get a bunch of shots in the—"

"Shut up!" Curtis yelled, nearly choking on the words. "It weren't no animal, or possum, or nothin' like that. It was a person. I think they got killed. We gots to call the police."

"Hell no, we ain't calling no cops," Willie said. "You done got blood on you and they'll think we did it. They'll throw us in jail for a hundret years or stick us in the 'lectric chair."

"No, they won't," James corrected. "We're just kids. They can't do that to us. Besides, they'll know we didn't do it. Hell, we might even get a reward or get our pictures in the paper."

"Yeah, I know what we'll get," Willie ventured. "We'll

get our hides tanned. Mom's warned us bout goin' in these old houses."

"First, we got to make sure what's in there," James said. "I want to see it for myself. I ain't calling the police over some dead dog."

"It ain't no dog," Curtis said sternly towards James. "I know what I saw. Go on and look for yourself. Go ahead. I ain't goin back in there. Not for a gazillion dollars. Go ahead and leave fingerprints and stuff. The police will put you under one of those bright lights and beat you and make you say you did it."

"Okay, Okay," Willie said. "No one is making you go back in there. You wait here and we'll be right back."

"No way!" Curtis yelled, his eyes getting big. "What if the killer is still in there and he gets you next. I ain't waiting on you. I'm going home. I want to wash my hands and change clothes. I'm goin' to call the police and tell them to check the house, but I ain't given my name."

"Hey stupid," Willie called to Curtis. "They'll trace your call. They do it all the time."

"I won't stay on long enough for them to get no trace," Curtis explained. "I've seen it on TV. I'll jus' talk long enough to tell 'em there's a body in the house and hang up. You got to stay on for over a minute for them to get a trace."

"Why don't you jus' call from the pay phone at the store on the way home?" James suggested.

"That's what I'll do," Curtis agreed. "No one will know

then."

"Don't tell 'em nothin' about us," Willie added. "We didn't go in there. We didn't see nothin'." The idea someone might still be in the house also helped to change their minds about going inside and hanging around the area.

"Okay then," James began, looking at the house. "Let's head back. Curtis can call the cops if he wants and then go home and get cleaned up. Willie, you grab the cart and we'll put it back on the way. I don't want someone else stealin' it."

"Here's your hankie back James," Curtis said. "Thanks."

"No, you keep it," James said, putting his hands up after seeing his hankie with blood stains all over it. "I don't wants it no more."

"Me either," Curtis said, and threw it in the bushes as they quickly walked away from the house. Each one looking back from time to time. Curtis kept wringing his hands together as if he were still trying to wipe them clean. He did this all the way to the store where the three boys went in and while James and Willie got fruit drinks for them, he stood at the counter still trying to get any small spot overlooked off his skin. As soon as the drinks were paid for, James gave Curtis his and out they went to the pay phone.

"I don't think I can do this," Curtis said, as he started softly crying again. "I'm scared. I don't know what to say."

"Well, somebody's gotta do it," James said.

"Why?" Willie asked. "Why does anybody got to?

Somebody will find it."

"He's a person, not an it, and by the way, somebody already did," James answered. The other boys looked puzzled at James. "We did," he said, throwing up his hands and shaking his head. "Wouldn't you want to be buried and have some preacher say somethin' nice about you instead of rottin in some old smelly house alone and your family not knowin' what done happen to you?"

"I'd rather not get kilt in some old house at all," Willie said. "And besides, he may not got no family. He might have been homeless. Maybe it was an accident. Maybe he fell and hit his head."

"No, James is right," Curtis said, his crying subsiding to sniffles. "I wants to call. I'll make it quick. I don't want him layin' there too long. Whoever he is, or was, he deserves better." He took a deep breath. "Okay, let's do it. I'm ready." The boys walked over to the pay phone and Curtis picked up the receiver, wiped his eyes with his other arm and again took a deep breath as he dialed 911.

CHAPTER 4

"I just talked to Starling," Gillam said to Lovett, as he hung up the phone on his desk. "He says the autopsy is almost done on Jessie; however, the final lab reports won't be back for a few days, if that soon. He got the Medical Examiner to do a rush job on her because of the weirdness of her death. The doc did say it looks like an overdose. No evidence of foul play was found, but some things just didn't look right."

"How so?" Lovett asked.

"Well," Gillam said, "it seems most of the main blood vessels in Jessie's body, if not for a better word, exploded. In other words, she was a walking hemorrhage."

"Jesus!" Lovett exclaimed. "You mean she suffered a massive stroke? I've heard about first time users doing something like that, but Jessie was a full-blown junkie."

"Yeah, there's more to it," Gillam continued. "The doc said it didn't happen all at once. It was like slowly blowing up a balloon too far until it popped, and it wasn't just in one spot. She was dead before they all burst, and it should have stopped once her heart stopped beating, but then again, there were signs the process continued for a while after she was dead."

"How's something like that even possible?" Lovett asked. "Once her heart stopped pumping wouldn't the blood stop and start pooling in the lowest gravitational locations? At least that's what they taught me in the academy. What's it called; lividity?"

"Maybe you should have been a Homicide Detective," said Gillam. "It's definitely weird. Maybe it's an X-file."

"You watch way too much TV," Lovett laughed. "You definitely need to get a life. You and your flying saucers, little green men from Mars, and Bigfoot. You're too much sometimes. Are you sure you didn't escape from some mental hospital or something?"

"You just wait till *you* see one too," Gillam said. "Then you'll be sorry and apologize, wishing someone would believe *you*. And they're not little green men, they're gray. And they *don't* come from Mars. At least, I don't think they do."

"Sure. Whatever you say," Lovett replied. "They come from billions and billions of miles away," doing his best Carl Sagan impression, which was regrettably bad. "And they come in peace. With super technology, eliminating world hunger, and medicines to cure all the world's diseases."

"It's possible," Gillam theorized. "However, it's a little too late for Jessie. Whatever the heck it was she got hold of."

"Yeah. Let's just hope they didn't bring some kind of outer space drug with them. That's all we need. Some out of this world, super extraterrestrial drug dealers."

"You're right about that," Gillam agreed. "We've got too many of our own right down here on Mother Earth."

"Yeah. But then it gives us job security," Lovett said,

smiling.

Gillam just laughed and shook his head at his partner. "Well, in a couple more hours, we can head home. And I don't mean out there," pointing into space.

The telephone on Gillam's desk began to ring and Gillam answered it. "Narcotics, Gillam here."

"Hey Gillam, how's it hangin'?" The voice on the other end said.

Before Gillam could answer, the voice Gillam recognized as Jack Simmons, one of the 911 operators and department techno geeks, continued to babble. "What was it that caused the hooker to take the eternal celestial dirt nap? Was it a murder or did she OD? Was she naked when you found her? What was—"

"Hold on, Simmons," said an exasperated Gillam. "We still don't know a whole lot and it's still under investigation by Homicide. There's nothing I can tell you right now."

"Okay, no problem, but if you hear something, let me know."

"You'll be the first," Gillam lied.

"Oh, by the way," Simmons remembered, "I don't know if it's related or not, but some kid, at least it sounded like a kid, called 911 a little while ago and said something about a body in an abandoned house. A patrol unit went by and now is calling for Homicide, and he also asked me to contact you guys."

"Okay," said Gillam. "You did. So, did they say why they wanted us?"

"The patrol unit checking the scene said he knows the dead guy there and he's a homeless junkie who frequents his beat. There's some drug paraphernalia there as well. He said he was at the scene of the dead girl earlier today, which is only a couple blocks away, and it reminded him of that. He's a rookie. Only been on about six or seven months and maybe he's just trying to make brownie points with you guys."

Gillam covered the phone's mouthpiece with his hand and called over to Lovett. Lovett was preoccupied with a report and Gillam threw his pen at him. Gillam could hear Simmons in the receiver, "Gillam, you still there? Gillam!"

"I'm still here," Gillam answered, as he pointed to the phone while Lovett rubbed the top of his head. He covered the mouthpiece again and didn't hear anything Simmons was saying.

To Lovett he said, "Call Homicide, see what they have and who is responding to–, where did you say the location was, Simmons?" cutting him off in the middle of a sentence.

"It's 1275 Griffin Street," Simmons replied. "You going over there? Let me know—"

"Yeah, sure," Gillam said as he was hanging up the phone.

"1275 Griffin," he told Lovett. "Looks like they may have another junkie who is taking the eternal cel—, crap. Now I'm sounding like Simmons. The rookie, what's his name? Adams? He came upon another body only a couple of blocks from the store where Jessie was found. It could be the same type of situation."

"I hope not," Lovett said with some dread in his voice.

"Let's go ahead and start rolling that way."

Lovett got on his radio, confirming Homicide was on the way to 1275 Griffin Street, and found out it was again Starling who would be handling the call. He let them know they would respond to the scene as well.

Lieutenant Jones also came on the radio and advised he would meet them at the scene.

"Great," Lovett exclaimed. "That's all we need today. Why can't he just stay away and play with himself?"

"Maybe he wants to see what real police work is like," Gillam said. "Besides, he's probably too sore already. It's not as if he has anything else to do all day. He passes off all the important work as well as all the everyday paperwork to the sergeants. He disappears for hours doing who knows what. I don't mind him out of our hair, it's just as a supervisor, well, he sucks."

"As a person, he sucks," Lovett added. "Hmmm, maybe that's what he does all day."

"As I've said before, Lovett, you're sick; however, you may be right."

When Gillam and Lovett arrived at the address, they needed to park several houses down due to all the police and emergency vehicles parked in front of the location. They also noticed Lieutenant Jones arrived ahead of them. They were not too thrilled. They were really hoping to avoid him today; like most days. As Gillam and Lovett walked up to the abandoned house, they met Officer Adams on the sidewalk.

"Hey, detectives," Adams greeted them. "Thanks for coming out. I thought you might want to see this after what happened with the girl earlier. I'm not sure if it's the same thing, but there is some drug evidence present. Your lieutenant got here very quick as well. He ordered me secure the outside and wait on the Homicide unit. He got here a few minutes before you did and went inside to meet with the lieutenant."

"Thanks," Gillam replied. "We'll check it out."

When they got up on the front porch, Starling came outside and met them.

"What is it with your jackass lieutenant, anyways?" Starling inquired, obviously frustrated.

"What did he do now?" Gillam queried.

"He's trying to take over the scene before we can make any determination about the guy's death. I don't know if he was murdered, if it was an accident, if he died of natural causes, or OD'd like your girl did over on Lowery Boulevard. He just came on in to the area and started walking all over evidence and even tracked through some blood. He left his shoe prints and possibly covered up and destroyed a murderer's or a possible witness's shoe prints which were left there first. I told him to get out of my crime scene and he just laughed and said 'you *think* it's yours' and then ordered *me* to go wait on you guys outside."

"I'd rather go to the dentist for a root canal than to deal with the lieutenant," Lovett said. "I've already checked with some of the other Homicide Detectives and if he turned up dead somewhere with a bullet in his ugly head, they said they would just stay at their desks and work from the report. They'd never be able to solve it because there would be too many suspects."

"Plus, they would call an animal control unit to pick up the body," Gillam added.

"He treats everyone under him like dirt and he's *sooo* great and can do no wrong," Lovett began. "He probably sits in front of a mirror at home and polishes his badge; calls his answering machine to hear his own voice; Pays different women to call the office to make it look like he likes girls. Goes to —"

"It's about time you guys showed up," Jones interjected, walking out of the house. There were no indications Jones overheard anything. "I've already called for the ME to pronounce and remove the body and I let the Crime Scene photographer go on to another more important call. Looks like some homeless guy tripped in the dark, hit his head and bled out. It was an accident, nothing more. No need for you to stay, Starling. I'm sure you have more important things to do as well."

"I'll need to contact my supervisor on this, lieutenant. I don't think he'll be very happy about having —"

"I've already spoken to Sergeant Moore, Starling." Jones interrupted. "In fact, he thanked me for saving you all the paper work. Goodbye."

Having been dismissed like a servant, Starling turned and cursed a red streak all the way to his car. He knew better than making a scene with a superior officer, but boy, did he want to strangle that S.O.B. It might even be worth it.

He would get with his supervisor, Sergeant Moore, and find out what the hell was going on. Surely something could be done.

Lieutenant Jones directed both detectives into the house and showed them where the body was located.

"I don't know why they always wear so much even when it's hot," he said. "And the smell! Is that him or did something else die in here last week? I just don't understand why some people want to live like that."

"Some of these homeless people don't have much and they carry everything they have wherever they go so it doesn't get stolen," Gillam explained. "Many of them don't have a choice about how they live. Some have mental or dependency problems and no family or anyone else to turn to. A lot of them are veterans with post-traumatic stress."

"Thanks for the social lesson, Mother Theresa," the lieutenant said. "I need to get into some fresh air before I throw up."

They walked out onto the front porch. "Okay, guys," Jones said, "I want you to wait outside here for the ME. Don't touch anything and don't go snooping around. This was just an accident and nothing more. No need for a big investigation or anything and there's no sense wasting too much time on this. Clear?"

"Then why do you need us to stay?" Gillam questioned. "The patrol unit can handle it from here if that's all you want."

"I want you to handle the report. As I said, it's an accidental death. Some no-name homeless guy without any identification on him. Most likely the old fart was too drunk or too high or both and fell over and struck his head. Died from the fall or bled out. Case closed."

"What do you mean, 'case closed'?" Lovett asked, exasperated at the lieutenant's attitude. "What makes you so sure about how he died or even when? Who is he and why was he in here? Whom do we notify? There are too many unanswered questions. And besides, why have us do the report when Homicide was here to start with and now, the beat officer is still here to do the report and can stand by for the ME himself?"

"There is no investigation for Homicide," Jones said. "I want you to write it up as an accidental death on this 'John Doe', black male in his 50's, and release the body to the ME when he gets here. Now, that's an order, sergeant! If you have a problem with it, then see me after you have it done."

Lieutenant Jones began walking back towards his car, handed the rookie cop back his flashlight he borrowed, got in his car, wove his way through the other vehicles in the roadway and sped off.

"What the hell was that all about?" Gillam asked, with a look of bewilderment on his face.

"I don't know," Lovett answered. "Maybe it's another 'screw you' job the lieutenant wanted to put on us. I've never seen him want to clear a case so quickly before. A questionable one at that. One which doesn't belong to us. There's no sense in it."

"Well, he may want it closed quickly, but I'm still going to check it out. I've got a funny feeling about this."

"I'd make a joke about your *Spiderman* senses, but you're not the Lone Stranger here. It has me wondering too."

Both detectives went outside and over to Adams.

"Tell us what you found," Gillam told the young officer.

"I got a radio call to check this house for a possible body. There wasn't any other information. I check the abandoned houses around here all the time to see if there are any homeless people or junkies hiding out. The patrol sergeant has us checking all the places they hang out and rousting them," the officer continued.

"I knew this house was unsecured and sometimes used as a shooting gallery and smokehouse. It's been like this ever since I got this beat."

"Who owns this place? Lovett asked.

"I don't know who the owner is," Adams said. "I get to know some of the regular homeless guys and try to keep them out. I got inside and saw this guy with my flashlight. I've seen this one before a few times. He's one of the regulars, but I don't know his real name. I know his nickname is 'Boomer'. There was blood all around his head and it didn't look like he was shot, or hit, or anything like that, and I recalled the way the girl looked earlier today."

"You told the dispatcher about some drug paraphernalia? Gillam asked.

"There were a couple small bags of crack and a metal straight shooter near him," Adams stated. "There were a couple of empty bags too. I checked him to see if he was still breathing even though I knew he was dead, I called my supervisor and he told me to call Homicide and the ME and secure the scene. I called radio on my cell phone and asked the 911 operator to call you and see if you wanted to come out."

"You did well," Gillam praised the young man. "What did you do with the bags of crack and the straight shooter?"

"I left everything just the way I found it," the rookie said.

"I didn't see any bags, or a pipe," Lovett stated.

"Neither did I," Gillam added. "Let's have another look. Adams, show us where you saw the drugs and stuff."

Adams led the detectives back into the house. Using his flashlight, he directed them through the house to a back room where the body was and began scanning the floor.

The detectives could see large red footprints on the floor throughout the room. Some went to the window and back and then faded as they headed out of the house.

"It looks like the lieutenant tried to paint the floor with the bottom of his shoes," Lovett said, shaking his head.

"What an idiot!" Gillam returned.

"It was right here," the bewildered officer said, pointing with the beam of his flashlight towards the floor next to the body. "I know it was here. And the pipe was right there too. There were three or four bags of crack. There wasn't anyone else in the house who could have gotten it. I checked it good after I found the body just in case someone was hiding. Somebody must have moved them after I came out of the place."

"Besides you, who else went in the house before we got here?" Gillam asked.

"Just your lieutenant and the Homicide Detective," Adams told them.

Gillam and Lovett looked at each other with that look long time partners know instinctively.

"Okay, we'll check with them," Gillam said, looking back at Adams.

"Maybe they picked it up as evidence. I'll tell you what; we'll handle this from here. I'm sure you have other calls to handle and we'll be in touch if we need anything further. You did a good job again"

"Thanks," Adams said with a smile. "My sergeant did want me to hurry up. Calls are backing up. Glad I could help. Will you keep me informed about what's going on?"

"Sure," Lovett said. "Call us anytime we can be of any

help with anything. It's good to see someone eager to learn."

The rookie walked back to his cruiser with a big smile on his face and thoughts of making detective sooner than he originally thought.

"There's the ME," Gillam said, pointing out to the street, as a black, box-style wagon, with Fulton County Medical Examiner written in big white letters on its sides, drove up the street towards them. "Let's clear the scene of the body and once everyone is gone, we can check out the area a little better without probing eyes or interference."

"Okay, but if there's any more evidence around, it's probably been stepped on, removed, or won't be of any use for anything."

"Yeah, I know. I just want to ease my mind on this some. Maybe I'll get the feeling of being a real investigator again for a while."

"Now don't go too far," Lovett laughed. "A man has got to know his limitations."

"That's great," Gillam returned. "Coming from a guy who has to use a step ladder to make a slam dunk into the waste basket."

"Oh, now that's funny," Lovett said, not laughing. "I might be a little short, but at least I don't have to chase a cat for some female companionship."

"Don't knock it till you've tried it," Gillam challenged.

Doctor George Kim was the Deputy Chief Medical

Examiner for the county and performed the expedited autopsy on Jessie. He approached the house where the two detectives were waiting.

"Hey, guys, what's up?" greeted Kim.

"Hi, Doc, "Gillam said. "Thanks for the quick job on the girl who OD'd. I still have a few questions though when you have time."

"What brings the Deputy Chief Medical Examiner out alone on a routine call like this?" Lovett asked.

"We're very short handed right now with all the cutbacks we've endured, I can't even get the AC fixed in the wagon," George explained.

"I have one associate on vacation," he said, as he held up one finger; "One out sick," holding up another finger; "One working on an autopsy as we speak," holding up a third finger; "Plus, the Chief is not due back until tomorrow from a conference," holding up yet one more finger and began wiggling all four fingers.

"Our office assistant is out on maternity leave, *and* I'm trying to train a new orderly to handle the intake, processing and office duties, so, I am obliged to pull up the slack and get my well-trained hands a little dirty with the field work. The office is starting to back up a little and it may take just a while to catch up. If you Narcotics guys don't stop bringing me more customers than Homicide, it will take a lot longer."

"Well, these aren't your routine shootings or stabbings,"

Lovett offered. "Is there anything new we haven't got word on yet?"

"You're right," the Doc agreed. "It's the strangest overdose I've ever seen. I don't know of anything new out there. There may be more to it than meets the eye and I'm doing some more checking. I have some samples I'm going to send to the State Crime Lab. You think this guy died the same way?"

"It's possible," Gillam said. "The rookie who just left found the body and said there was some crack and a pipe, and then somehow, right after Lieutenant Jones left, the evidence came up missing."

"So, what are you trying to say, Gillam," Kim asked. "Jones took the dope? I've known him for years. He's an ass, but then again, I didn't think he was like that."

"I'm not trying to say anything yet," Gillam stated. "I just don't know what happened, but I won't let it rest either. If he took it and I can prove it, I'll burn him."

"I understand," Kim replied. "I won't shed any tears for him, but do you really think he took it for himself or what?"

"To tell you the truth, I just don't know," Gillam said. "I don't think he's using, and then on the other hand, he has been acting strange for a while now."

"He's always acted strange to me," Lovett added. "However, he's been more on the weird side lately. Like today, showing up where he's not needed and giving strange orders."

"He's trying to get too involved with simple cases or

cases which aren't even ours. Last week when a patrol unit made a traffic arrest and some crack was found on the guy, the lieutenant showed up at the scene. I just happened to talk with the officer involved later in court and he told me about it," Lovett continued.

"The lieutenant also did a field test on the dope and get this, he even offered to turn it in for him. The officer hadn't even called for a Narcotics unit. The lieutenant just showed up out of the blue. The officer was running late so he gave the lieutenant the dope after he packaged everything and filled it all out."

"Maybe he was just driving by and wanted to see if the officer needed some help," Kim suggested.

"It's possible, but have you ever known him to 'offer' to do someone else's work?"

"Not in this life. Did he turn in the dope?" Kim asked.

"As far as we know, but you can be sure we're going to check," Gillam said.

"Well, I better get the poor stiff and get back to the office," Kim said. "I just hope I don't run out of fuel with him in the back. That would be embarrassing. Someone forgot to fill up the old meat wagon and I didn't have time to stop on the way here. I should be able to make it though. I'll get our new orderly to fill it up after I get back. As soon as I get the results back from the State on your girl, I'll let you two and Starling know what's up. I wish I could tell you more about her, but it's something I've never dealt with."

"Thanks," You need some help inside?" Gillam asked.

"If you don't mind helping bag him, getting him up on the gurney, and then loaded into the wagon," Kim asked, "I would be grateful. I'll be able to handle it from there, I think. I'll get you each a pair of latex gloves, some shoe covers, and a mask."

"How about some air freshener while you're at it," Lovett said. "It's bad enough to gag a skunk in there."

"Welcome to my world. Here, try this," George offered, handing him a small jar of Vick's Vaporous. "Put just a little under your nose, not in it. It should help some."

"Always prepared, I see," Lovett stated."

"I was a Boy Scout. Plus, you learn real fast after your first time. Now, I never leave home without it."

"If this keeps up, I'll need to buy some too," Lovett added.

"Let's hope it doesn't come to that," the ME said.

"That's for sure," Gillam said.

William N. Gilmore

CHAPTER 5

Lieutenant Jones arrived back at his office shortly after 7:00 p.m., shut the door and drew the blinds to keep wondering eyes out. He reached into the pocket of his sports jacket and removed several small plastic, zip-locked bags containing small white chunks of crack cocaine. He also removed a short aluminum tube with a burnt smudge on one end and put the paraphernalia on his desk.

I wonder who's missing a radio antenna from their car today, he said to himself. He sat down at his desk, unlocked a drawer and removed an envelope from it, placing the pipe and packets of cocaine into it and sealed the envelope. He threw the envelope back into the drawer next to several others just like it and then locked it back. *That may come in handy later*, he said, with a silly grin on his face.

He then removed his billfold from his back pocket, opened it and took out a small folded piece of paper. He unfolded it and began to dial the telephone number which was the only thing written on it.

"This is Jones," he said, when the connection was made. "Another one was found by a rookie cop on Griffin Street. I got there in time to take care of all the evidence I could find before someone else got hold of it. What do you want me to do now?"

There was silence for a long time on the other end of the phone and then a voice said to Jones, "I told you not to call this number unless it was an emergency. You call this an emergency? You take care of things for us. You don't get to ask questions. You don't interfere. You get paid. You screw this up, you get dead. Is that pretty clear?"

"Yeah, no problem," Jones said, trying to keep his voice from quivering; the silly grin disappeared. "I was just trying—"

"We know all about it," the voice said. "We keep tabs on everything. Don't let your guys get too nosey and keep things running smooth. Make sure those bodies are taken care of."

Jones heard the click on the other end and the line went dead. With his hands shaking, it took him twice to get the telephone handset back on the cradle of the base.

It took a couple minutes for him to compose himself before he headed out. He believed he needed to prove his usefulness again. He formulated a plan.

The Deputy Chief Medical Examiner got the body secured in the wagon and went back into the house to check with Gillam and Lovett before taking off.

"Anything else I can do for you guys?" He asked.

"Not here," Gillam stated. "However, if you don't mind, keep us posted along with Homicide on the test results and let us know if you hear anything about any other similar deaths."

"I'll do it," Kim answered. "It may take a couple of days.

I've got a backlog right now and I have a couple of priority cases which must be done first. Doing the girl today put me behind and I got this call before I could write up the report."

"We understand back logs," Lovett returned. "And we appreciate you getting to her as soon as you did and if you don't mind, let's keep this just between us for now. Something strange is going on."

"I'll do what I can. It does look like the same thing though. What's going on anyway? Is there something I'm not being told?"

"I don't think any of us are being told everything," Gillam said. "Even if there is something going on, we're being kept in the dark."

"Just like mushrooms," Lovett added. "Kept in the dark and fed B.S."

"Well, I hope I can shed some light on it for you guys," Kim said.

"Thanks," Gillam said. "You're not as bad as they say you are."

Kim gave a puzzled look at the detectives and asked, "Who's *they*?"

"You know," Gillam said. "It's the *they* who talk about what you do with the bodies at the morgue in the middle of the night. Especially the young, pretty, well built, dead girls."

"Don't you start that crap with me or you won't get

anything on this investigation until next year," said an exasperated Kim.

"Okay, Okay," Lovett said, laughing. "He was just kidding. No need to get your bowels in an uproar. I'm sure you get kidded enough about working at that place. I sure wouldn't want to do it."

"Why not?" Kim asked. "The benefits are great, and you don't get any complaints from the customers." Then he smiled and winked at the detectives as he turned and walked back to his wagon. He drove off waving out the open driver's window.

After the ME left the scene, Gillam told Lovett, "I'll check outside if you want to check in here."

"Okay," Lovett paused. "I'm not sure what I'm looking for though. If I knew for sure what the heck was going on it would be a lot simpler."

"Just use your imagination. It could be anything," Gillam shrugged. "You just don't know."

"That's true," Lovett agreed. "I'll go get my flashlight from the car and give the house the once or maybe even the twice over. I'll give a holler if I find anything."

"Same here. Be sure to check out those shoe prints the lieutenant left behind. And see if you can find anything with a name on it. And don't forget to check—"

"Do you want to do the inside too?" Lovett interrupted.

"Sorry about that. I know you know how to do your job, but I don't want to overlook anything."

"I tell you what," Lovett said. "After I get through in the house, why don't we trade, and you can check it out? It's what we usually do when searching rooms in a drug house for dope."

"Good idea, but we better hurry. We've only got about an hour or so left before it's time to go home."

"What's wrong Larry, got a hot date with a kitty?"

"No," Gillam stated. "However, there is a new UFO special on tonight."

"Oh, brother," Lovett said, shaking his head. "You have *got* to get a life."

Lovett returned from the car with his flashlight and began a search of the house while Gillam began checking the outside. Gillam got around to the window which opened into the room where the body was found. On the ground, just a few feet from under the window, was a large piece of plywood which appeared to have been covering the window at one time. Gillam lifted the plywood and saw two small red handprints on the other side.

"Hey, Lovett," Gillam yelled inside the window.

Lovett walked into the room, "Jezz, Gillam, you scared the crap out of me. I must have jumped a foot when you yelled."

"Come out here and look at this," Gillam said.

"What'd you find?" Lovett asked, as he walked to the window.

"Come out here and see," Gillam answered. "You can't see it from in there."

Lovett went back out of the room and a few seconds later came around the back corner of the house. There was Gillam, holding the large piece of plywood which he leaned up against the house, stood back a few steps and stared at.

"What do you make of that?" he asked Lovett.

"Are those hand prints?" Lovett asked, squinting at the board.

"There, you see, I *will* make a detective out of you yet. And who do you suppose made those hand prints and why are they red?"

"Well, I believe the prints were made from blood, possibly blood from the body, and the prints are so small, I would say they are from a small woman or a child."

"And I would say, 'BINGO', on both counts," Gillam exclaimed. "Simmons told me the tip about the body possibly came from a kid. I bet he was in here playing and found the body and somehow got his hands bloody, then pushed out the board either to see better or to get out that way."

"You think he may have been in here when Adams came in to check the house?" Lovett asked.

"No," Gillam said. "Adams said he checked the house. I think he had been gone a while. I bet he's the one who called 911. We'll get a transcript of the tape and an address the call came from. Maybe we'll get lucky. I don't think he was involved with the death; however, he might be a witness to something. Let's take the board with us just in case though. I think it will fit in the trunk."

How come there weren't any small footprints in the house?" Lovett inquired.

"Because they were covered up by big footprints. And I want to know why."

"Sounds like you may have found that spark you were looking for," Lovett said with a slight grin. "There may still be an investigator in there after all."

"It's a start, anyway," Gillam agreed. "Maybe it will turn into something we can sink our teeth into and take a good bite out of Jones. I'm not sure what's going on, but I bet somehow, he's got his dirty little hands deep into it."

"I agree," Lovett said nodding. "Let's go finish up some of this paperwork and get the heck out of Dodge for the day and get a fresh start tomorrow. I'm bushed and you've got your close encounter tonight."

"Sounds like a plan to me," Gillam agreed as they walked back to their car. "Sure you don't want to beam over and watch. You might learn something."

"I don't want anyone to know I associate with that kind of freaky stuff and those kinds of screwballs."

"Hey," exclaimed Gillam. "I'm not a screwball."

"Yeah, right," Lovett answered.

The plywood board just did fit into the trunk of the detective car. They transported it to the police property section where Gillam took a swab of the blood on it before covering the board with brown paper and logging it in as evidence. He sealed the swab into a plastic, zip-locked bag. Afterwards, they went up to their office and Gillam began the incident report for the lieutenant's approval.

"Why don't you go ahead and get out of here," Gillam told Lovett. "I've got everything under control with this, and I'll be leaving pretty quickly myself. I want to turn in the blood sample from the board anyway. It's on the way home."

"Thanks, I think I will. I've had enough of this place today and if I don't leave, then I can't come back tomorrow. And I just can't wait to get back here tomorrow," Sam said.

"You have the logic of a Vulcan," Gillam smiled.

"And may the frigging force be with you too," returned Lovett with a laugh. "I'll see you tomorrow," he said as he headed for the door giving a wave behind him.

"Give Deb a kiss for me. The dog too."

CHAPTER 6

Gillam was just walking out of the Narcotics office when his telephone began ringing. He debated about going back to answer or letting his voice mail pick up and getting the message, if any, tomorrow. It was a short debate and Gillam got to his phone on the fourth ring.

"Narcotics, Gillam here," he answered.

"Larry, it's Sam. I've got some bad news. Kim, the ME, is dead. Died in an accident on the way to his office with the body from Griffin Street."

"You're kidding," Gillam exclaimed. "What happened? How'd you find out?"

"Heard something on the news about the accident and called the ME's office. I didn't get any answer, so I called Grady Hospital. Secondhand information I got was the wagon left the roadway, hit a tree and caught fire. The whole thing burnt up with Kim inside. I just hope Kim died on impact instead of from the fire."

"Jezz. Any other cars involved or any witnesses?"

"I don't know. I didn't get to talk with the investigating officer yet, but I think it's our next move."

"I'll stop at Grady on the way home and check it out."

"You want me to meet you there?" Sam asked.

"No need. I'll give you a call at home if there's anything up. I didn't know Kim very well. Do you know if he has a family?"

"I know he was married and I think there were a couple kids," Lovett said. "I recall once he said something about sending for his wife's mother in Korea to come visit or live with them, something like that."

"What a shame," Gillam said. "Anyway, I'm leaving the office now. I'll let you know something as soon as I can."

"Right," Lovett returned. "And if you need me, just call."

"Got you." He hung up the phone and headed out the door.

Gillam arrived at the Grady Hospital emergency area and parked his personal car in an area where there was a good chance of getting a ticket or being towed. He checked in with the security guard at the emergency entrance showing his ID and asked if he knew anything about the ME's accident. The older than dirt rent-a-cop was about as bright as his faded and crusty badge. "I don't know nuttin' bout no accident. What's a M-E?" he asked.

"The Medical Examiner; you know, the Coroner, the guy who tells you how somebody died," said a bewildered Gillam. The guard looked even more confused. Trying to match something with the guard's age, he said, "You ever watch *Quincy*? Okay, never mind. I'll find someone. Thanks anyway."

"No problem," said the guard.

Gillam walked into the hospital shaking his head. *Chief material*, he thought. He came across a nurse who was a lot more helpful and directed him to an Emergency Room treatment area and to ask for a Doctor Szalkoski. Gillam went to the treatment area the nurse indicated and saw a doctor listening through his stethoscope to the upper back of a young man. Gillam waited until the doctor was through with the patient and about to walk out and asked if he was Doctor Szalkoski.

"That's me," said the doctor. Gillam introduced himself and asked if he was familiar with Kim. "I pronounced the death, DOA," the doctor stated nodding. "I was unable to tell the cause of death due to the condition of the body. I guess someone in his office will need to do that. He was released to the ME's office about a half-hour ago. His wife and mother-in-law were here at first, and I think they went over there as well."

"Thanks a lot, doctor. Oh, and by the way, what can you tell me about the other body in the ME's wagon? Was it sent over as well?"

"What other body?" the doctor asked, looking very puzzled. "They only brought in one from the accident. No one said anything about another person brought in. Could they have been taken somewhere else?"

"It was a previous incident victim Kim was transporting. Maybe it was taken straight to the ME's office. It was being brought in from another case I was handling when the accident happened."

"Oh, that's a relief. I wish I could help you," said the doctor, "but I only know of one person being brought in. I do know the officer writing up the accident is in the nurse's station. He asked me several questions earlier and I know he spoke with Ms. Kim, but that's all."

"Thanks," Gillam said. "I'll go see if he's still there."

"Good luck," the doctor wished the detective.

Gillam headed down the hall and around the corner to the nurse's station, and asked if the officer was still there. The nurse directed him to a back office and Gillam met with Officer Wilson who was apparently working on the report. Gillam introduced himself and explained what was going on.

"I'm sorry, detective," the officer started. I just came to Grady to do some follow up for the officer on the scene and only stopped to pick-up the victim's wife. There's another unit still out working the accident. I don't know if there was another car involved or not," he said, shaking his head.

"I've been in radio contact with him and he said because it was a Fulton County vehicle involved, there's a county unit out there also. They're out with ID units from both jurisdictions taking pictures and doing a dual investigation. I don't know too much about what they might have found. I had to go to the house of the victim, Mr. Kim, and do the notification to the wife and bring her to the hospital. It's an ugly job."

Gillam nodded. He remembered how it was.

"You can't tell them their loved one is dead," the officer continued, "only that they are needed at the hospital. They keep asking, but you tell them you don't know anything. I think she knew though. There were kids there too and she was able to get a neighbor to take care of them," his voice quivered just a bit.

"She and the older lady, maybe her mother, who came with her, were talking in Chinese, Korean, or something and both were crying half way here. You just don't know what to say at that point, so I said nothing. I'm glad the doctor told them. I don't think I could have. I got another unit to take them to the ME's office while I finished here."

"I know what you mean," Gillam said. "You say the vehicle is still at the scene of the accident?"

"Yeah, as far as I know. I hear it was pretty messed up. The other officer did tell me it took a while for the fire department to put it out. He said it appeared to have caught fire after it hit the tree and rolled. All the gas going everywhere caught the grass on fire and pieces of metal were everywhere. It took a while to get the guy out of the cab after they got the fire out. I think everything on the inside was destroyed."

"Okay, I get the point. I'll head over to the scene and find out what's going on. Where is it?"

"It's at the 1200 block of Armour Drive," the officer said.

"Armour Drive? What the heck was it doing on Armour Drive?" asked Gillam, surprised. "He was on his way to the ME's office from Griffin Street. That's over six miles in the wrong direction and in a run-down commercial area which has been mostly abandoned as well."

"I can't tell you, detective," the officer said. "I don't know anything about what was going on before the accident."

"I know," Gillam said. "I don't expect you to know. I'm just asking myself questions I don't even have answers to either. At least, not yet."

Gillam left the hospital and was going to head towards Armour Drive. He decided to stop at the ME's office over on Pryor Street first. It wasn't very far away and he wanted to at least pay his respects to Kim's family. In addition, He wanted to talk to whoever brought Kim's body back.

Gillam entered the ME's office and saw his partner Lovett sitting and talking with what appeared to be one of the orderlies in the main lobby.

"What are you doing here, Sam?" Gillam inquired, with a bewildered look.

"Hey, we're partners, aren't we?" Lovett asked, with a grin. "I was just getting ready to call you. I'm not about to let you get any glory without me."

"And if I screw up?" Gillam asked.

"You're on your own. What's your name again?" Lovett said, with a straight face which was just beginning to crack.

"Thanks a lot," Gillam said. "What have you found out here?"

"This is Jaccob Mutumbo. He's the only employee here now. He's here on a diplomatic sponsored grant to learn to be an ME's assistant in his country. He's the one who brought Kim's body back from the hospital." Mutumbo stood to greet the detective.

Gillam reached out to shake Mutumbo's hand and it was immediately swallowed up like the night. Gillam craned his neck back to look up at the six foot, eight-inch giant. He was wearing a white lab coat which was much too short for him.

"It be good to greet you," came from Mutumbo in such a strong African accent, Gillam needed to think for a second to put the sounds together to understand what he was saying. Mutumbo was pumping Gillam's hand and arm like an old-fashioned water pump and grinning with teeth so big and white, that for a second, Gillam thought of the Cheshire Cat from *Alice in Wonderland*.

"It's my pleasure. I wish it could be under other circumstances, Mr. Mutumbo," Gillam said.

"You please to call me Jaccob," said the orderly. "Mr. Kim did. He was my friend. He help me with my English and he show me things. I bring him back from accident. He be gone from here now."

"He's not here?" Gillam almost shouted out. "Where is he?"

"He be with Father, Son and Holy Ghost, Amen," Jaccob said, crossing himself. "He be in a better place now."

"Yes, yes, of course," said Gillam, glancing over at

Lovett who tried to hide the smirk on his face. "I understand he's gone to Heaven, but where is his earthly body?"

"His shell be in the back," said the big man softly. "His wife and other woman be there. I let them have time with Mr. Kim's shell and tell them he is gone to his reward, amen."

"Okay then," Gillam said, not wanting it to sound sarcastic. "What about the other body, the one which was in the back of Kim's wagon?"

Mutumbo gave the detectives a funny look and said, "No other shell. Mr. Kim alone. You are making fun with Jaccob," giving a wide, bright smile again.

"I wish we were," said Lovett. "We helped him get the body, the shell, into the wagon. Is it possible it completely burnt up? That it's only ash?"

"I don't think so," Gillam said shaking his head. "There should be something left. We'll go out to the scene and check it out ourselves."

"What about Mrs. Kim?" Lovett asked.

"I don't wish to bother them right now. I'll check about the arrangements later and maybe we can send some flowers or something. Unless you think there is an urgent need to question Mrs. Kim, I think we can wait until after she's had some time."

"We can wait. Hey, Jaccob, would you happen to know if Kim has files on the young black girl brought in earlier today from Lowery Boulevard? The name should be Jessie Ryder."

"I will look in box where papers are," Jaccob said,

walking over to a row of filing cabinets. "I help Mr. Kim get her shell and bring it here. Mr. Kim teach me much."

After just a few minutes looking, Mutumbo shook his head and said, "No, no papers for Ryder today, I not file papers for Ryder. Maybe Mr. Kim has them in Mr. Kim's room."

"Do you mind if we look?" Lovett inquired. "They are very important to us."

"We go to Mr. Kim's room and look see," said a determined Mutumbo, and the detectives followed right behind.

They arrived at a door with 'George Kim, Assistant Medical Examiner, Please Knock' on it. Either out of habit, respect, or just being literal, Mutumbo knocked on the door; of course, no one answered.

Mutumbo tried the knob and the door opened to a dark office. "Door mostly locked when Mr. Kim not here," he said. He stepped out of the way and allowed Gillam to enter and Gillam reached over to the wall searching for the light switch. Just as he felt the light switch plate, a large hand grabbed his wrist in a tight vice.

William N. Gilmore

CHAPTER 7

"Do not move," Mutumbo said.

Gillam couldn't move even if he wanted to. Lovett begun backing up and put his hand on the grip of his semi-automatic.

"Something not right. Smell, see, feel, not right. Petrol in air," Jaccob said in such a whisper, it could have been mistaken for the wind. There was no smile on his face.

Gillam couldn't smell anything, and he sure as heck couldn't see anything. The only thing he felt was Mutumbo's big hand around his wrist.

"You can let go anytime now, Jaccob," he was about to say. However, he only got out "You —" when Mutumbo tightened on his wrist and said, "Shhhh." Mutumbo gently pulled Gillam out of the doorway and back into the hallway, slowly closing the door. When the door was finally shut, Mutumbo let go of Gillam's wrist.

"What the hell is going on here, Jaccob?" Gillam exclaimed, while rubbing his wrist.

"Is someone in there?" Lovett demanded, not taking his hand from his gun while keeping an eye on the door and Mutumbo at the same time.

"Someone been there, not Mr. Kim. Room not safe now," Mutumbo said, in a matter-of-fact tone. "How you say, 'boody trap'. Petrol bomb go 'boom' if light turn on."

"Booby-trapped?" Gillam almost shouted.

"Booby-trapped?" Lovett repeated. "With gas? What are you trying to say Jaccob? There is a gas bomb in there ready to go off if we try to turn on the lights? Is there someone in there now?"

"No one there now, but before," Mutumbo said. "Petrol smell high, near top. Maybe light bomb. Another person smell, not Mr. Kim."

"How do you know this, Jaccob?"

"I was soldier for country. Now, I am soldier for God."

"Okay, let's say you're right for now," Gillam said. "Do you have a flashlight, Jaccob?"

"Yes, I go and get. Do not go in room. I be back," said the big man.

"We'll wait right here then, Arnold," said Lovett with a grin. That's just a joke. You know. Arnold Schwarzenegger. '*I'll be back*'."

Mutumbo just stared with a blank look on his face.

"Okay, I'll explain it later," Sam said as he shook his head.

Jaccob turned and continued after the flashlight.

"What do you make of that?" Lovett asked.

"I don't think he sounds anything like "The Arnold," Gillam said, with a smirk on his face.

"No, you idiot, I mean about a gas bomb in there," Sam

said, pointing towards Kim's office. "You think there is one? I thought he might be kidding us."

Gillam got very serious. "I don't think he's kidding. My wrist doesn't, anyway. He's too straightforward, too intense about this. I didn't smell anything; however, I don't have a nose that big nor the elevation. If there is one, we better get the bomb squad out here pronto. We might have some explaining about what we're doing here though."

"If there is one, I want someone to explain to me what a bomb is doing in Kim's office in the first place," Lovett said.

"It would be a good start," Gillam returned. "And then I want to know who this Mutumbo is. The comment about being a soldier has me wondering as well. Here he comes."

Jaccob was walking back with two flashlights, one in each hand. "I found the light," he said.

"Amen," Lovett said, and that big grin showed up on the orderly's face.

Jaccob handed the flashlights over to the detectives and said, "Slow!" in a long drawn out whisper.

"Don't worry," Gillam said. "I don't plan on being a customer here for a long time." Gillam and Lovett turned on their flashlights and Gillam slowly opened the door. With the light, they could see that Kim's office, as small as it was, held a desk and chair, a couch, and one filing cabinet. The filing cabinet drawers were open with papers hanging out and scattered all around the floor. The couch, probably used more as a bed for catnaps instead of sitting, was pulled away from the wall with two cushions knocked on the floor. The desk was a sea of papers all over the top and around it.

"It's been ransacked," Gillam noted.

"That, or Kim was extremely messy," Lovett ventured.

Mutumbo pointed up to one of the lights hanging from the ceiling. They were ordinary old-fashioned single bulb lamps. Gillam stepped in closer to get a better look one of them.

"Sam, look at this," Gillam said, putting the beam from the flashlight on the bulb. The reflection of the light on the bulb and the underside of the white metal shade made it almost too bright to look at. Sam could see the bulb wasn't translucent. Something was in the bulb and there was a small piece of silver tape, maybe duct tape, on the bulb near the metal screw top.

"It's gasoline," Gillam stated. "I can smell it now. Not much, just barely noticeable. I've heard about this before. If I turned on the switch, there would have been an explosion like a Molotov cocktail. Flaming gas would have been thrown all over, igniting the papers on the floor, the desk, everything, and this place would have been like an incinerator. Whoever turned it on would be like Kim right now. A crispy critter."

"You think it was meant for Kim, or someone else?" Lovett asked.

"I don't think it was meant for anyone special," Gillam stated. "My bet is it was done to cover up the search of Kim's office and destroy any evidence left behind, or that something was taken. Jaccob, did anyone else come in tonight?"

"No one come other than Mr. Kim's wife and other woman. I be only one here when Mr. Kim leave. When I go get Mr. Kim's shell, I lock door. When I come back, door still lock."

"That's when they came in," Gillam said, nodding his head. "They, he, or whatever must have picked the lock or used a key and came in after Jaccob left.

"You still want to call the Bomb Squad," Lovett asked.

"I'm not sure if it would be a good idea right now," Gillam answered. "I'm not sure if this has anything to do with what's been going on with those two deaths or not, but just the same, let's keep this quiet for now and see where it leads. Jaccob, can you reach up and safely unscrew the light bulb without touching anything else?" Reach up was the wrong phrase. Jaccob could touch the ceiling without going on his tiptoes.

"Yes, I go slow. Do not touch light," he said, pointing to the switch.

"Don't you worry about that," Lovett assured him, handing Jaccob his handkerchief. "Just keep it in the cloth and try not to rub it any more than you must. We might be able to get some fingerprints."

"No," said Mutumbo. "I use paper to get light out. Possible to make light go 'boom' if cloth rub light."

"Yeah, you're right," Gillam said, replacing his handkerchief. A static charge from the cloth could set it off. You know a lot about these things, don't you, Jaccob?"

Jaccob gave his big, white-toothed grin once more, but this time without saying anything. He picked up a piece of paper and then touched the metal filing cabinet to discharge any static he may have built up on his body. Reaching up with the piece of paper, he slowly unscrewed the gas filled light bulb. When the bulb was out, Jaccob kept it straight up and handed it to Gillam, who took a closer look at it. He lifted the piece of tape and saw what he expected. There, at the top of the glass, just before the metal screw part was a small hole.

"Look here, Sam," Gillam said, pointing at the bulb. "This is where the gas was put in. A pin or needle is heated until it can pierce the bulb in this area and then gas is put in the bulb with a syringe. Sometimes, black powder is used. The hole is then covered with the tape. It's a simple and deadly device, but you better know what you're doing. I think someone did, and it wasn't their first time."

"O.K., now that you have it, just what are you going to do with it?" asked Sam.

"Here, catch," Gillam said, making a motion like he was going to toss it to him.

Sam put his hands out in front of him, "Oh, no you don't. It's your baby. I wish the two of you all the happiness in the world. I should have stayed home. There are some days it just doesn't pay to be a nice guy."

"I think we ought to look around some more," Gillam

stated, "just to see if anything else is out of place or if there are any more surprises for us."

"I agree," Lovett said. "I think we should also take our early warning system with us. What about Mrs. Kim and her mother?"

"Oh, crap," Larry exclaimed. "I forgot about them. We should have gotten them out before we started fooling with this thing."

"Well, I understand where your mind was at the time," Lovett offered. "I just remembered myself. I guess we should get them out now before we or they come across anything else."

"Good idea; however, I don't want them to know what's going on. Hell, I don't know what's going on, but let's go ahead and get them out."

"Jaccob, could you tell them you need to close now, or you have to go out on a pick-up. Anything."

"I tell them I close now," Jaccob said. "I don't tell lie to them."

"Sure, just so they are out and safe," Lovett said. "I wish we were too."

Gillam looked for a safe place to put the bulb down. In the break room off the main reception area, he found a wide coffee cup he could set it in for now.

Mutumbo came out of the back area with Mrs. Kim and her mother. Both women looked like they spent the past couple of hours crying their eyes out. They probably had.

Gillam approached the younger of the two. "Mrs. Kim, I'm Detective Gillam and this is my partner, Detective Lovett." As she reached her hand out to shake theirs, she switched a tissue from one hand to the other.

"We want to say how sorry we are for your loss. If there is anything we or the police department can do, please, just ask."

"Thank you, so much," she said in almost perfect English, surprising Gillam. He hadn't known what to expect.

"This is my mother. I'm sorry, she doesn't speak much English." She translated what Gillam said to the woman into Korean and the elder woman began bowing her head several times to the detectives, saying something neither detective understood.

"She thanks you also and prays for your safe journey through this night, and the following days and nights to follow."

"Tell her we really appreciate it," Lovett said. "We could really use some extra prayers these days," he continued, while nodding his head and looking at Gillam. Gillam nodded his head as well.

"Are you handling the accident, my husband was in?" Mrs. Kim asked.

"No ma'am," Lovett said. "George was working on a case of ours, and we needed to pick up some files on it when we found out about the accident." There was no need to go into details with her about their investigation.

"May I call for a car to come by and take you home," said

Gillam.

"No, thank you though," Mrs. Kim said, pulling a cell phone from her purse. "I have someone coming by for us. I called earlier and they should be here very shortly. I must get home to the children. I have a lot of explaining to do." She began to cry again, quietly. "We'll wait outside for our ride, if you don't mind."

Gillam nodded his head. He didn't mind; in fact, he was relieved. Not just for their safety, but for his own emotional well-being. He could feel the tightening in his throat and a wetness building in his eyes.

"If you call or come by tomorrow," Gillam said, walking the ladies towards the door, "I believe the Chief ME will be back and can handle any arrangements you may need to have made." Gillam wanted to get the women out of the building as quickly as he could, but then again, as delicately as possible.

Mrs. Kim spoke to her mother again in Korean and the women began walking out as Gillam held the door open for them.

"Thank you again, detectives." Ms. Kim said. The elderly Korean woman also said something to them through a sorrowful half smile which would have been understood in any language. *Thank you*!

The women walked out to the parking lot, arm in arm.

"Very nice ladies," Lovett interjected. "What a shame. I'd hate for Debbie to get a knock on the door like that."

"Then you better keep your eyes open and your nose clean for sniffing," Gillam cautioned. "There's no telling what else we might run into in here. I doubt if there's anything else; however, you best be on your toes just in case."

CHAPTER 8

Gillam and Lovett, with the assistance of the orderly, Jaccob, began a slow room-by-room check of the entire ME's office. Luckily, they hadn't discovered any new booby-traps or evidence of any other pilfering so far. No other files or desks appeared disturbed in the area.

They finished with the front half of the building and began the check of the work areas in back. Again, slowly checking areas which might be affected, they would steal a look at Jaccob and watch as he put his nose to work. After checking areas and finding them OK, he would look at them and shake his head, indicating to them, to their relief, he could sense nothing.

Only one area was left to check. The refrigerated slide-out boxes where some of the bodies were stored before and after their examinations. Most were empty. Gillam and Jaccob checked the doors carefully prior to opening them. Once they were cleared, they would check the interior. After checking the empty boxes, they moved to the ones which were occupied. Lovett stood back and watched.

"What's wrong, Sam?" Gillam asked, with a smile. "Afraid one of them might jump out and get you? Want to eat your brain or something?"

"Nah, they just give me the willies. You go ahead and

have fun, I'll check around a bit."

"Don't go and get yourself blown up or I'll never talk to you again," Gillam said with a chuckle.

"That makes it awful tempting," returned Lovett. "However, I don't think Deb would talk to me either, and I'm not willing to trade good for bad."

Gillam walked over to one of the last doors and Jaccob said, "That one holds the shell of girl Mr. Kim and I bring back today."

Gillam opened the door slowly and when he saw nothing which looked like a booby-trap around the opening, he opened the door all the way.

"There's nothing in here, Jaccob," Gillam stated. "Are you sure she was in this one?"

"Yes, yes," Jaccob insisted, looking past Gillam and into the empty refrigerated space. "When Mr. Kim finished, I put her shell back in same space," pointing to the space where Gillam held the door open.

"Is there any place else she could be?" Lovett asked. "We know she didn't get up and walk away."

Jaccob checked the last remaining storage bins, but the body could not be found.

"You know," Lovett said, looking around the area, "this is getting to be too much like one of those 'B' movies with Bella Lugosi or Vincent Price. If I hear a wolf howl or see a bat, I'm out of here."

"Relax, would you," Gillam said. "There's something strange going on, but it's not supernatural. Ghost and vampires don't use gas bombs. The kinds of monsters we're dealing with here are flesh and blood."

"Those can be even worse," Lovett added. "So, what's the plan now? Do we notify someone, write up a report, or stick our heads in the sand?"

"I don't know who to trust right now, or which way to turn with this thing," Gillam said, giving a disgruntled look.

"Well, I vote to stick our heads in the sand," Lovett returned. "I know we can trust Starling. He could be a good start. Plus, I know he has no love for Jones so he already has points on his side."

"You're right there," Gillam agreed. "Let's get with him first thing in the morning and get a game plan going with this thing. I don't think there's anything more we can do tonight. I was going by the crash site, but I'm sure it's been cleaned up by now. I'll do it tomorrow when it's light. I'll wrap up the light bulb and put it in my garage for safe keeping."

"You don't have a garage anymore." Sam reminded him, shaking his head, "You live in an apartment now. Remember?"

"Yeah, you're right," agreed Larry shaking his head as well. "Sometimes, I just plain forget. Must be that old-timer's disease."

"Don't worry about it. I'll take it with me," offered Lovett.

"Jaccob, we need you to keep this quiet for now," said Gillam, turning to the big man. "We need some time to try and find out what this is all about. Do you have any problem with that?"

"No, Jaccob not have problem," the orderly said. "Jaccob think maybe you have problem."

"You can say that, again," Larry said.

True to his nature, Jaccob began to repeat what he just said.

Gillam stopped him before he got too far. "No, no, Jaccob, that's just a figure of speech. It means we agree with you, but just the same, keep your eyes and ears open." Gillam thought about what he had just said for half a second. "Which means be careful and watch out what goes on around you."

"God watches over Jaccob," the orderly said, with his big, white, grin flashing.

"Next time you talk with Him, how about putting in a good word for us?" Gillam asked.

"Jaccob will say many prayers for you."

"Thanks" Gillam said. "Will you be okay here for now until we can get someone else in here to handle the office and ME duties?"

"Oh, yes" Jaccob said. "I have much to do. I can put back papers on floor in Mr. Kim's room and take care of Mr. Kim's shell."

"Yes, you do so and call us if you find anything missing

or looks strange," he said handing Jaccob one of his business cards. "We'll have dispatch contact someone to come over right away, but don't forget what happened here is to stay quiet for now, okay?"

"Okay," Jaccob said, with a little puzzlement in his eyes. "I not want to lie to anyone. What about the other shell, the girl?" he questioned Gillam.

Gillam explained further to Jaccob, "We'll be looking into that, but right now we need to get more information about who set the booby-trap and why. We'll be able to do that better if we don't let everyone know what we've found and what we're doing about it. Do you understand?"

"Yes." answered the big orderly. "I know what you do. You do the Lord's work and like Him, you work in mysterious ways, for good."

"That's one way to put it," snickered Lovett, immediately turning serious. "Someone is trying to keep us from finding out the truth, and we need to know why and who it is. And Jaccob, we're going to need your help."

Jaccob flashed that big grin one more time and said, "It be good to do the Lord's work again."

Gillam wondered what other 'Lord's work' Jaccob may have done in the past and if it involved any of the skills he showed from his soldiering life.

"I guess we're done here for now," Lovett said. "It's late and we have a lot to do in the morning. I say we call it a night and meet up in the morning, check out the accident site and the ME's wagon, and then go from there."

"Sounds good to me," Gillam agreed. "I'm whooped and could use a good night's sleep. Let's get out of here. Good night, Jaccob, and again, we're sorry about Kim, but we'll get to the bottom of everything." Gillam started to reach his hand out to Jaccob, then thought better about it, and just gave him a slight wave. Lovett did the same.

As the two detectives left out of the building, Gillam asked Lovett, "Well, what do you think?"

"That's one big S.O.B.," Lovett said. "I wouldn't want to run into him in a dark alley some night. I don't think I'd have enough bullets."

"True," Gillam remarked, "but I mean everything else. What happened to Jessie's shell, I mean body," he said shaking his head. "And what about the accident? I'm not so sure now it was an accident."

"What do you mean?" Lovett wanted to know.

"Things just don't add up. Why would someone booby-trap Kim's office, and what were they looking for in there?" Gillam replied. "What about these deaths, and the missing evidence, and the way Lieutenant Jones is acting? I've got that feeling again, and you know what happens when that happens."

"Oh, yeah," Lovett replied. "Late hours, funny looks from the wife, and trying to keep you in line. I wonder if I can put another transfer in. This time I think I'll put one in for the Larceny Unit. I think working on old ladies missing social security checks would be better than having to baby-sit you and getting my butt chewed out every other day."

"Sure," Gillam said. "And where would you get your excitement? Playing solitaire or spades on the computer? You know you're better off with me. I make you a better detective, a better person."

"You're right," Lovett agreed. "I should divorce Deb and marry you. You've made me what I am today. Or maybe I should sue your ass for giving me high blood pressure, helping what little hair I have left to fall out, and making me neurotic."

"I think that may be Jones' fault, but let's not go there," Gillam said. "I'm too tired to get into all that again. I still have to stop at the Crime Lab."

The two detectives went to their cars and drove off from the parking lot not noticing the black sedan with dark tinted windows parked down the street. Even so, they would not have seen the figures inside watching them with binoculars.

William N. Gilmore

CHAPTER 9

Curtis' hands were covered in dried blood. He couldn't wipe it off no matter how hard he tried. He was in a dark house and there was a terrible smell. He looked down and his shoes were covered in blood.

Over in the corner, just barely visible, was a figure. It was standing. It began to moan and walk towards him. The first things he saw clearly were the outstretched hands and the blood dripping from the boney fingers. As the figure got closer, he tried to back up, but found he was soon against a wall with nowhere to go. The smell of rotting flesh was overpowering, and the figure kept coming.

As bad as he wanted to scream and close his eyes, he couldn't do either. The figure got even closer and as it was almost upon him, he could see the figure clearly. There was blood all over the head and face; however, he could still recognize his brother, Dante.

Curtis woke in a sweat and almost screamed for real. He sat up and looked around. It was still dark, but the specter of his brother was gone and the air was fresh and there were no signs of blood anywhere. He began to cry. Just little soft sobs at first and then he buried his face in his pillow.

It had been a long time since he dreamt about his brother

and he still missed him terribly. This was the first nightmare since shortly after the funeral. Every other dream was about the good times they shared.

Now, with the events of the previous day a lot of emotion came down on the young boy. He didn't know how to handle all this at his young age and he began to wonder if somehow his brother was sending him a message, if he angered some spirit, or if he brought all this on himself somehow. The only good thing was he didn't wet the bed.

He began to think about what type of message his brother might be sending if that was what it was. He felt bad about the body in the old house and how they just left it there. He did call the police and told them. He heard about all the police at the house later and wondered if he should have done more.

He didn't want to get involved and he was too scared to tell the police anything more, but what could it have hurt. He decided to think more about it in the morning. Rolling over, he tried to go back to sleep; however, too many thoughts were going through his head and he was afraid he would again see his brother covered in blood if he closed his eyes.

🔫

Gillam, as tired as he was, also had too many thoughts racing through his head to get to sleep. He thought about his two ex-wives and the divorces, little gray aliens, the two drug related deaths, Kim's accident, the big orderly, Jaccob, and of course, Lieutenant Jones.

Gillam, lying on his couch, was wondering how they all were related while the television flickered in the living room of his apartment. Cali was purring by his side with no care in the world and Gillam's eyelids started to fall. A commercial for a gasoline company came on and just at that time, Gillam's eyes flew open and he sat up causing Cali to jump down and look up at her human as if to say *What the heck's wrong with you?*

Gillam went to his phone and started to call Lovett, but then looked at the clock and saw it was almost eleven. "Okay," he said to no one, "it'll wait till morning." Gillam got some paper and a pen; went into the kitchen, sat at the small dinette, and began writing down some thoughts. He finally hit the sack about one. Cali beat him to it.

The ringing sounded as if it were underwater, getting louder as it rose towards the surface and then, as if it was surgically implanted in his head. Gillam rolled over towards the nightstand and picked up the phone. "Hello," he said hoarsely, with his eyes barely open and his tongue dry as a desert at high noon.

"Good morning, Sleeping Beauty," Lovett teased. "Rise and shine."

"Screw you," a drowsy Gillam said. "What time is it?" Not wanting to open his eyes fully to look at the clock.

"Time for you to get your fat butt up. It's after nine," Lovett lied.

Gillam squinted his tired eyes, peered at his alarm clock, and saw it was almost seven. "*What* time is it?" he asked, not sure what to believe.

"All right, so it's only seven," Sam confessed. "Time for you to get a move on. We have lots to do and I want to get started early. Can you be ready in, say, a half an hour or so and meet me at the office around eight?"

"Sure. I should be able make it by then. Just have a donut and a soda waiting for me and pull up a copy of Kim's accident report, will you." Larry asked, as he pushed himself up from the bed.

"Ah, breakfast of champions," Lovett said. "Your wish is my command. Just don't forget to pay me back sometime. See you there."

Gillam took a quick shower and shaved, fed and petted Cali, and was on his way within thirty-five minutes. He made sure he grabbed the notes he jotted down last night. There were still many questions to be asked and answered; however, he felt he was on to something and couldn't wait to share his theories with Lovett.

Gillam entered the Narcotics office and saw a box full of mixed donuts, and a soda on his desk. "What's all this," Gillam asked Lovett, who was at his own desk.

"You didn't say what kind of donut you wanted, so I got a few for you to choose,"

"A few," Gillam said, opening the box of donuts.

"There's enough here to choke an elephant."

"Remember, *you* said that and not me," Sam laughed. "Just save me one or two."

"Get your own," Larry said. "You had your chance and you blew it."

"Naw, I wolfed some down earlier with my coffee," answered Lovett. "You usually beat me in here. Have a late night with the cat?"

"No, I did some thinking about all this crap going on and I came up with some ideas I want to go over with you, but first let's get out of here and head over to where they towed the ME's wagon."

"Sure," Lovett said, handing him the printed out copy of the accident report. "I thought you wanted to go out to the accident site first."

"We'll get to it later. There's something I want to check out with the wagon first. If I'm right, then we may be in deeper than I thought. And I'd rather not talk around here. I'm not sure whom to trust anymore or what words might get back to you-know-who. And I think it might be a good idea to keep an eye on each other's back more closely than we ever have before. Not trying to scare anyone, but you may want to tell Deb to be aware of anything suspicious too," cautioned Gillam.

"You really think it's gone that far?" Lovett questioned him with a hint of foreboding.

"If what I think is going on is," Gillam answered. "I'm

afraid so."

Gillam and Lovett arrived at the impound yard where the
ME's wagon sat after being towed. Gillam met with Mr.
Granger, the supervisor at the yard and asked about it.

"Yeah, it's here," Mr. Granger said, "but I was told by
Lieutenant Jones not to let anyone near it. It was involved in a
fatal accident."

"Yes, we know," Gillam said. "We're looking into the
accident."

"Well, he told me to call him if anyone tried to see it, but
I don't guess that means you guys. He was kind of an asshole
about it too. It all seems kind of hush-hush. Aren't all you guys
with Narcotics?" Granger inquired.

"Eh, yes," Lovett replied. "However, we can't go into
details now. We're trying to pin this one down because it was a
friend of ours who died in the accident. And yes, Lieutenant
Jones is an asshole; the big hairy kind. One reason why we're
trying to stay a step ahead of him on this."

"I'm sorry to hear about your friend," Granger said,
sounding as if he actually meant it. "Just tell me what you need.
I'll be happy help you guys out and as for the asshole, I didn't
see you by the way."

"That's great," Gillam said with some relief. "If you
could just show us the wagon we'll get out of your hair as quick
as we can."

Granger escorted the two detectives to an area where the wagon was separated from other impounds. There they saw a mass of charred crumpled metal. Nothing was recognizable to show the purpose of the vehicle. All the tires were melted. The front end was smashed on the left side and it looked like the wagon rolled over a few times.

The fire department used the 'jaws of life' to get into the cab of the wagon to get Kim's body out. The cab was badly burnt, inside and out. The air bag had been deployed; however, it was mostly burnt away. The back doors were forced open by the crash with one of the doors off lying next to the wagon. There was a strong odor of gasoline still present. Fire had gutted the back compartment as well.

"It took a lot of damage," the man said. "I don't see how anything could have survived that. Was your friend alone in the wagon?"

"As far as we know," Gillam said. "He was supposed to be transporting a body back to the ME's office when the accident happened. The wrecker driver who picked up the wagon at the accident site, is he here today?"

"He doesn't work until this afternoon. The wagon was his next to last pick-up last night. Do you want me to have him call you when he gets in?" Granger asked.

"Sure," Lovett said, giving Granger one of his cards.

Gillam tried to get into the back of the ME's wagon, but it was too unsteady and too dirty with soot and ash from the fire.

He didn't see any evidence of charred human remains or that a body ever occupied the back. No bones, charred skin, melted pieces of body bag, nothing. If they didn't know better, they would swear there had never been anyone in the back.

Gillam went to the side of the wagon and saw the gas door flap was closed. Upon opening it, he found the gas cap missing. From the looks of the plastic cord which once held the cap, and the dirt around the gas port, it had been missing for a while. However, that's not where the gas odor was the strongest. Gillam tried to get down to where the gas tank was located and could just see the tank. It looked intact to him. No leaks or pools of gas, He asked Granger if he could borrow a long screwdriver or long piece of metal with a sharp tip. Granger went off for a few minutes to try to find the requested tool.

"What's up, Larry?" Lovett questioned with a frown.

"Remember when Kim picked up the guy in the house? He said he was almost out of fuel and just enough to get back to the ME's office and have the orderly go fill it up.

"That's right," Sam agreed.

"But the accident was over on Armour Drive. In the wrong direction to his office from the Griffin Street pick-up and there aren't any gas stations in that area either."

Granger returned with a long rod of metal with a sharp tip. "Will this do?" he asked.

"Very nicely, I believe," Gillam said, taking the piece from Granger. "Now if you both will stand back a bit, I *think* I can do this without blowing us all up."

"What are you about to do?" Granger inquired, backing away, with a frightened look as if the metal rod Gillam held was a snake.

"I just want to check the gas tank," Gillam said as he got down on the ground again. He then took the metal rod, jammed it into the upper part of the tank, and hit the end with a rock. It took him several tries before he finally pierced the tank at the top and when he pulled the rod out he heard the slight pressure release of the fumes from the tank. He then pierced the lower part of the tank the same way and out came a small stream of the liquid which soon turned into a trickle and then to a slow drip.

"I got the answer I needed," Gillam stated.

"So, what does that prove?" Granger asked, furrowing his brow.

"It was just an experiment," Gillam told the man. "I just wanted to see how much fuel was left in the tank.

"I get it," Granger said, nodding his head. "I'm no country bumpkin. The fuel tank didn't rupture. The gas came from somewhere else. Someone torched the wagon after the accident. You've got an arson on your hands."

"That's possible," Gillam answered. "We've got some work to do, so if you'll excuse us, we'll be on our way and don't forget, mums the word. Right?"

"No problem," Granger said, as the detectives walked away, got in their car and drove off the lot. Granger hurried to the office and got on the phone. When the other party answered, Granger said, "Hey, Doris, you're not going to believe what I found out today, but you've got to keep it quiet, okay?"

No one noticed the dark sedan pulling out of a side street and begin to follow the detectives.

CHAPTER 10

As they drove off the lot, Lovett said with some alarm in his voice, "I don't believe what happened to Kim was an accident. We've got more than arson; we've got a murder. I think our next move is to check the so called 'accident' scene and talk with the investigating officer."

"You're right," Gillam said, nodding his head. "Someone poured gas all over the outside and inside of the wagon and set it off. The fire didn't reach the fuel tank and there wasn't enough in the tank to go off and although there were some vapors in the tank, I think they forgot to check the fuel cap and with it missing, the vapors were able to slowly escape before building up too much pressure. Not a real expert job, but almost good enough. There's one more thing they forgot."

"What's that?"

"The Medical Examiner's wagon runs on diesel, not plain old gasoline and diesel burns different from gasoline. Smells different too"

"Jezz, you're right. I could still smell gasoline all over the outside of the wagon even before you opened the fuel tank. It looks like someone may have disabled or killed Kim somehow and then staged the accident. But why all that just to steal a body? What is going on and who do you think is involved?

Jones?"

"I'm not sure, Sam," Gillam said, shaking his head. "If Jones *is* involved, he can't be acting alone. For one thing, there's *too* much going on and second, he's not smart enough to do anything of this size by himself. I don't know what the motive is, but whatever it is, it's enough for someone to commit murder, set a bomb which could cause more death, the destruction of possible evidence, and who knows how much more."

"One thing for sure," Sam added, "we've got to watch our backs like you said. We've talked to a lot of people and asked most to keep things quiet. You know how difficult that's going to be. The word will get out about our questioning people involved in this thing somehow and very soon, I would expect. Maybe it's time to take that vacation Deb and I have been planning. You should think about one too."

"That's not my style; however, it might not be such a bad idea for you Sam," Gillam returned. "If things around here get too hot, I'd say maybe it's time for you and Deb to look at starting over elsewhere. It's not worth it for you to stay. No case is worth your life."

"If things do heat up, I'll think about sending Deb to her mom's, but I'm not leaving you here by yourself. We're a team and we have a job to do. 'Don't let the suckers get you down.' Isn't that what you've always told me? We're the good guys. Let's go kick some ass!"

Curtis wasn't in a mood to play today. For one thing, he didn't sleep well. In fact, after his nightmare, he didn't sleep at all. When he came out of his room early this morning, his Aunt thought he was sick and told him to stay in the house today while she was shopping. Curtis thought it might be a good idea. He didn't want to see anyone today. As the morning wore on, Curtis desperately trying to force himself to stay awake, fell asleep for little cat naps while lying on the sofa watching the television.

Once, while waking up from one of the short naps, he thought he had been dreaming of his brother again after hearing moans and seeing someone with outstretched hands walking towards him. At first, he was startled, then saw it was just one of those zombie movies on the tube with one of them wanting to eat someone's brain. It was enough though to get him thinking again. He soon talked himself into believing everything happening; the nightmares, the body, were signs telling him to do something or to tell someone.

Curtis believed if he told someone at the police station what happened, it would all go away. There were no friends there to influence him into changing his mind this time and there was nothing scarier than the nightmare, not even the police. Curtis went over to the phone and with a deep sigh, dialed 911.

ᕽ

Sergeant Starling answered the phone in Homicide and on the other end was operator Simmons.

"Hey there, Sarge," Simmons stated with undue

familiarity. "I've got what sounds like a kid on the line who says he was at that house over on Griffin Street where the body was found yesterday."

"Oh really?" Starling countered. "And how do we know he's telling the truth?"

"I'm not the detective. I just pass along the info for you guys," Simmons stated. "You want the call or not?"

"Okay, Simmons, patch it through," said an exasperated Starling.

Starling heard a few clicks and then herd Simmons tell the kid to go ahead.

"Hello," said a young and shaky voice.

"Hello, I'm Sergeant Starling. I understand you were at a house on Griffin Street yesterday. Why don't you tell me what you want to say. Oh, wait a minute. Thanks, Simmons, you can go now." There was no reply, just a loud click.

"Okay, now, can you tell me what your name is son," Starling asked, afraid there would be another loud click on the other end.

"It's ah …, it's ah …, John," stammered the voice.

"Hello, John," Starling said with a slight smile he was glad the kid could not see. The type of smile from knowing a lie when you hear it. "There's nothing to be scared about. I'm here to help. It's what I do. I'm sure you've been told in school that policemen are here to help, so that's what I'm going to do. Can you tell me why you were in the house yesterday?"

"Some friends and I was playing, looking for stuff. You know, to play with." *Maybe I shouldn't have told him about the others*, Curtis thought for a second and then continued. "I went in this house and there was this dead guy, all bloody and stuff. I didn't do it, I promise."

Starling could hear the shakiness in the kids voice as if he was about to start crying any moment.

"No, no. I know you didn't do it. I think it was a drug overdose that killed him. He did it to himself. You just found him later."

"That's right," Curtis said, with some relief. "I couldn't hurt no body. I ain't like that. When my brother Dante got killed I swore I wasn't gonna be like that. I don't do no drugs or belong to no gang or nothin' like that."

Starling was jotting down a few things and now he had something to work with. He got the attention of one of the other detectives in the office and gave him a note to run some info on another computer while he continued the conversation.

"How old are you, John?" Starling inquired.

"I'm, ah, fifteen," Curtis lied.

"Okay, John. I'm going to tell you something. Do you trust me?" Starling asked. "It's important you trust me, John."

"Yes, I trust you. You're a policeman."

"Good," Starling said. "My name is John, too. And I can tell sometimes when someone doesn't tell me the truth. It's important I trust you as well. You are telling me something and I need to believe you. If you lie to me about part of it then the whole thing is a lie. Isn't that right? Don't you want me to believe everything you are telling me?" Not waiting for an answer, Starling continued. "I think maybe we should start from the beginning and trust each other. Don't you think that would be a good idea? Let's say we forget everything up to now. Would that be okay?"

"Okay," Curtis said, and he began to cry a little. "I'm sorry. I was scared. I was told you'd arrest me."

"Now, that's not true. You didn't do anything wrong. In fact, I'm sure you called to help. Okay, let's start all over again," Starling said, with as much passion and empathy he could muster. He felt bad for the kid. He had his own reasons for relating to the hurt the boy felt. Reason's that some on the department might know. And very few whom he confided the truth about what really happened.

"My name is John, what's yours?"

There was silence for a moment and Starling thought he may have lost the kid after all and he would hang up.

"It's Curtis," the kid said, turning that moment into a young man. "I'm sorry I lied. I want to do the right thing."

The other detective brought over a sheet with the 911 info on it concerning the address where the call originated and info on a Dante killed two years ago with the same last name from that address. Starling said to Curtis, "I'm sure your brother would have wanted you to do the right thing too. Your brother, Dante, was killed two years ago by a gang's drive-by shooting, wasn't he?"

"How'd you know that?" asked Curtis. "You *did* trace that call I made yesterday."

"I can't tell you all our secrets, yet," Starling said. "But maybe someday, if you have a mind to do so, study hard and stay out of trouble, you might be a detective yourself."

"Wow, really," said a truly excited Curtis, forgetting for the moment the reason he called in the first place.

"Sure, you're just what we need on the department. We have a junior program for kids. I'd love to come talk to you about it if that would be okay with you and your mom."

"I live with my aunt. She's kind of old, but I think it'd be okay. Also, I lied bout my age. I'm almost nine though," he said with some pride. "I jus' want to tell the truth now."

"That's a good thing," Starling stated, also with some pride in keeping the kid on the line along with getting him to tell the truth. Maybe there was even a slight chance of keeping the kid straight. "Now is there anything you can tell me about the house, the guy, or anyone hanging around in the area that seemed strange to you?"

"The house sure did stink! I don't remember nobody hangin' round and nobody else was in the house. And I didn't touch them drugs."

"What drugs?" Starling inquired.

"I remember there was some drugs next to the guy. I

didn't think bout that till jus' now. I jus' hardly saw 'em. Some cocaine in some small bags and a stem, you know, a crack pipe. I jus' saw 'em, I didn't touch 'em."

Starling remembered Lovett telling him what a rookie patrol officer observed prior to his arrival and after Lieutenant Jones got there. It bolstered the case that Lieutenant Jones for some unknown reason removed the drug evidence. He thought he better notify Lovett and Gillam about what he was told and maybe they would want to question the kid too.

Starling verified Curtis' address and telephone number and told him he would call later when his aunt was home and he would tell her how he was helping with a case and not in any trouble.

Curtis knew she would think the worst if the police called the house without any reason. He hoped she would overlook him disobeying her by going in the old house, but then would be proud he was helping the police and maybe someday be a detective himself.

CHAPTER 11

Gillam answered his cell phone on the second ring. It was Sergeant Starling. He relayed the conversation with Curtis Harris and agreed that Lieutenant Jones must have picked up the drugs prior to his arrival. Why he didn't tell anyone was just speculation at this point; however, there were a lot of theories going through everyone's head, and not one of them was good. Gillam agreed to get with him later to go and talk with the kid in person. Maybe they could learn something more.

Gillam just hung up with Starling and repeated the information to Lovett when his phone rang again. He felt like answering it 'Grand Central Station', but instead just gave his usual at work "Narcotics, Gillam here" answer.

"Detective Gillam, this is Granger over at the impound lot. Have you or your partner heard from my wrecker driver, Thompson? He's the one who picked up the Medical Examiner's wagon."

"No." Gillam put his phone on speaker for Lovett to hear as he turned towards Sam and just mouthed "Granger".

"Neither have I. He didn't show up for work and I can't get in touch with him. He still has the wrecker out. It's not at his trailer and there's no one there. He has his moments, but he's never done anything like this before and he's worked for me for five years. Could I get you to check this out for me? I don't know if it's related to your case or not, but it's mighty suspicious."

"Were pretty busy right now," Gillam returned. "If we get a chance to do so, we'll come by and see what we can do. That's the best I can offer right now, unless you want to make a report on a stolen truck and I'll transfer you over to Auto Theft."

"Oh, no. Not right now. I want to give him a chance in case he went out and got himself snookered somewhere, or met up with some hooker, or something like that. There's always a first time I guess."

"Okay, I'm sure that's the case. Let us know if he shows up before we get by or if there's any other word."

"Thanks," Granger said, concluding the call.

"Now that's something, isn't it," Lovett asked.

"What's that?"

"A wrecker driver has a life and you can't buy one."

"Don't start on that this morning. I've got too much to worry about already without you on my case about something that's none of your business anyway. Do me a favor and let's just focus on work today. Things will go a lot smoother."

"Touchy this morning, are we? All right, I'm sorry. I guess it's my way of relieving some stress too. You're right. Let's just worry about this crap for now and then we'll have some time to relax. Maybe we can go on that fishing trip, or even go hit the casinos. Who knows, maybe I'll even go to one of those science fiction conventions with you."

"That'll be the day. Who's out of touch with reality now?" Gillam snickered.

"You want to head over to the accident scene now?"

"Yeah, that's next on my list. I want to see if things add up with the way the wagon looked and the accident report. Then if we need to, we can get with the investigating officer and the fire-rescue unit."

The detectives arrived at the Armour Drive site of the accident and could see the scorched grass where the Medical Examiner's wagon ended up. The tree it must have hit was about fifty to sixty yards away and closer to the street in a curve. The grass was torn up in-between and that's where the wagon flipped over.

There was still debris scattered around and there were numerous tire tracks in the grass leading up to the area. Obviously, some of the tracks were made by the wrecker removing the wagon, the fire trucks and possibly other emergency vehicles.

Gillam went to the tree, saw a large gouge in it, and saw some branches scattered around that the top of the wagon must have hit and knocked down.

In all appearances, it looked like the wagon was going around the curve too fast, left the roadway, and clipped the tree with the left front, turning over and flipping several times. For it to have done that though, it would have been going at least twenty to thirty miles an hour or more over the speed limit of thirty-five. No other car, as far as it could be determined, was involved and there were no known witnesses.

"This was a very low traffic district and no reason for anyone to have been hanging in the area," Gillam said to Lovett.

"The real problem I see," Lovett said, pointing, "is that the wagon was headed *away* from the Medical Examiner's Office. Why?"

"There would have been no reason for Kim to be headed in this direction or at that speed," Gillam said. "Not unless someone was chasing him."

"That doesn't make any sense," Lovett said, shaking his head. "Who would be chasing Kim? And again I ask, why?"

"You answer that and you might have a whole new case," Gillam surmised.

He checked the roadway for some distance and didn't see any fresh skid marks. He did find some tire marks on the curb where the wagon may have left the road. It was just about the right angle to hit the tree as it did. It didn't look like Kim tried to stop the wagon before leaving the road. Maybe he couldn't.

Lovett was checking the area around where the wagon came to its final resting spot. The area was still wet although there hadn't been any rain since the accident. A lot of water must have been used to put out the fire, he thought. There was also the faint odor of gasoline still. And the odor of the burnt tires. There was even some of the burnt rubber left on the scene. Gillam took some of this, placed it in a zip-lock bag, and put it in the trunk of their vehicle.

"Find anything?" Lovett asked, as he walked back to Gillam.

"I took some samples of the burnt tires that smelled like gas just in case there's anything we can do with them. How about you?"

"I don't think so. Everything looks like it should, according to the report. I did get an odor of gasoline over by where the wagon ended up, so I guess that's where it got poured on. There aren't any types of surveillance cameras, traffic cameras, or even ATM cameras in the area, so we don't have any video or photos at the time of the accident. There are no witnesses to speak of and the way our luck is going, I'm not even sure the rats around here will squeal."

"Now, that's bad!"

"Our luck, or the joke?"

"Both."

They headed back and got into their vehicle and Gillam started the car. "Did you see it?" He asked, Lovett.

"Yeah, the black sedan sitting up the road. I was wondering about that. We're being watched."

"I think it followed us from the impound lot," Gillam surmised. "I picked it up a couple miles back, but wasn't sure. Thought I was getting paranoid. Now, I'm sure. What do you want to do?"

"Can we back up five yards and punt? I'd like to confront them, but either they'll run, or we might have a shootout right here. Furthermore, we don't know how many are in there and how well they're armed. I'm not ready to show all my cards now by trying to get someone else to stop them. Maybe we should just pretend we didn't see them. Lead them on a wild goose chase."

"I think your right about not tipping our hand, but then again, I don't want to get caught out in the open either, under manned *or* under gunned. Let's just start heading back to the office, see if they follow us and we'll see what happens from there. We've still got a lot of work to do and maybe we can make those calls we need to if the lieutenant isn't there."

"Sounds like plan 'B' is in the works. Drive on Miss Daisy," Lovett said, trying again to release a little stress. It was hard to do so as he pulled out his Smith & Wesson 9mm, checked to make sure one was chambered and held it in his hand as they began to drive out of the area.

In a short while, they got back into regular traffic. They were still several miles from the office and Gillam kept a lookout for the vehicle following them.

"Yep. It's there. It's keeping its distance, but able to stay with us through lights and traffic. They're good."

"Any possibility there's more than one?" Lovett asked, trying his hardest not to turn around and draw attention.

"I don't know. I'm too focused on driving and trying to keep an eye out and make sure they don't drive up and ambush us. I don't know if they have any orders to take us out or just follow us. I've got an idea though. Call dispatch and get hold of Simmons. Get him to monitor the traffic cameras on Peachtree between 14th Street and Ponce de Leon. I'm going to head that way and have him see if he can get any pictures of the car and hopefully a license plate."

Sam called and got Simmons on the phone. He put it on speaker for Larry to hear. Sam didn't go into a lot of details, but told him they needed some information from the live feed traffic cameras. After a few minutes, Simmons reported he was watching a bank of about 20 cameras on his monitor and was waiting for further instructions.

Gillam then headed down Peachtree and passed the first monitored intersection as Lovett gave Simmons the information on their tail.

"I got you," Simmons said. I've got about ten or twelve cars crossing the intersection now. Okay! I've got your bogey about seven or eight seconds behind you. It looks like a dark colored four door sedan, maybe a Ford or could be a Lincoln or similar type vehicle. You want me to call you some back-up?"

"Not yet. Can you get a license plate number?" Lovett asked.

"No, the camera angle is bad at that point. I'll keep trying."

Gillam kept driving down Peachtree, hoping they wouldn't get caught at a light just in case it was an ambush, while Lovett continued with Simmons.

Simmons pried a little more, trying to get Lovett to tell him what was going on.

"Do me a favor, Simmons. Just help us out here. We don't have time to explain everything. This is important. *Real* important. That's why we called *you*," Lovett pleaded, trying to stoke his ego a little.

"I understand," Simmons said, sitting a little straighter in his chair. "I won't let you down. Okay, now I've got you crossing 7th Street," he continued. "Your tail is still about the same distance and I've got other cameras here to help and …, there it is! I've got the plate! I can't tell you anything about the occupants. Windows are too dark."

Lovett asked Simmons to run it to see what registration came up. He bet it would come up stolen.

Gillam wanted to make sure there was only one tail and told Lovett to have Simmons check the cameras at 10th Street. He said he would turn right once he got there then head up to one of the gas stations and pull in. There would be witnesses and cameras there if needed.

They made the turn on 10th Street and headed up half a block to a station on the right. They pulled into the lot just as Simmons told them the tail did not turn, but continued on Peachtree. However, a black van turned onto 10th, pulled over, and stopped. No one got out of the van.

Gillam and Lovett went into the store, leaving the line open just in case. They bought some sodas, returned to their vehicle, and pulled out, onto10ᵗʰ Street. Right after they pulled out, the black van pulled off continuing up 10ᵗʰ Street.

"You've got a new tail," Simmons gave the bad news and the description. "I was able to get the tag on the van when it stopped."

"Who are these guys," Gillam asked, as he headed back toward the office. "What do they want?" He sounded frustrated and angry at the same time. "I'm about tired of this game. We're close enough to the office now. Let's have some fun. They want to play tag. They're it."

William N. Gilmore

CHAPTER 12

"Hey, I've got some bad news for you guys," Simmons began.

"The car is stolen, isn't it?" Lovett interrupted. "I knew this was going to be harder than it looked."

"No," Simmons continued. "The car doesn't show stolen, but there appears to be a government block on the registration. You know, like it belongs to the FBI, or the CIA, or some undercover unit. I can't get anything to come up and I'm sure it's been flagged that someone is trying to check it out."

"How about the van then?" Sam inquired.

"It's the same. There's nothing on it. Just a block on the registration site when I try to run it. That's why I think it's some government thing."

"Okay, then. Do us a favor and try to keep an eye on us till we get back to the office. We're only a few minutes from there and see if you can monitor the van and see where it goes or if the car shows up again. Thanks, Simmons."

"No problem guys. Anytime. Just keep me in the loop."

"Sure. We owe you that much," Lovett said, closing his phone.

"What are the Feds doing checking us out? Lovett asked. "Did you forget to pay your taxes, Larry, or could it be the *Men in Black?*"

"Now's not the time, Sam! This changes things a little. It might be the Feds. It might not. Still, we need to be careful. We're going straight back to the office. We need to find out what's going on."

"And how are we going to do that? Call up the local Federal Bureau of Intimidation Office and ask them. I don't think so. You know how it works. They don't release *any* information. Nada. And if it's some kind of black ops, then no one will know about it anyway. Right now, all we have is each other. Is there *anything* you haven't told me? Any secret things in your past such as being a spy, having a Mafia Godfather, or being an alien? Anything?"

"No, Sam, it's not me," Gillam said, getting more frustrated. "I could ask you the same damn things. I don't have a clue. Not unless it has something to do with this case. That's the only thing I can come up with. I don't know what we've gotten ourselves into."

"Maybe it's Jones. Could he have someone checking us out?"

"I just don't know. We've got a couple off days coming up and maybe things will quiet down. I don't know what else to tell you."

"That's the first time I've seen you like this and *that's* what makes me scared."

"To tell the truth, I'm a little scared too. It's not knowing and not being in control. I hate not knowing. I hate not being in control even more. I don't want to feel like a puppet on a string. Especially if Jones is the one holding the strings. We need to get to the bottom of all of this. It could mean our jobs."

"It could mean our lives." Lovett said with concern. "So, where do we go from here? What's our next step?"

"Follow plan B. We continue to the office, make some calls, get as much information as we can, cover our tracks and our butts, then we put it all together and see where it leads us."

"I've got one more thought." Lovett said as he grabbed a note pad and began writing something on it. When he got through and Gillam got a chance to read it, it read:
What if we've been bugged? The phones, the car, our homes?

Gillam just shrugged. What could he say at that moment? If they *had* been bugged, then anything he said about the note would give it away that they knew. If they abruptly changed the subject to anything else, that also would give them away. He then got an idea.

"Ah, crap! Gillam said, with Lovett looking over at him with a surprised and bewildered look. "You see what that pigeon did to our windshield." Gillam looked over at Lovett and was motioning him with his right hand. "Now look, the wipers have just spread it all over and I can't see crap."

"Well, pigeon crap anyway," Lovett said, catching on and nodding his head.

"That won't come off with just the wipers," Gillam

continued the charade. "We'll need to take it through a car wash now. There's the one just over by the office we get to go through for free."

"Yeah, it's time to get all this crap washed off," Sam started almost too loudly. Gillam giving him a funny look as to say 'What are you doing? Keep it real.'

They arrived at the entrance of the car wash and there were only a few cars there as they pulled in line. Gillam showed his badge to an attendant and signed a ticket for the free car wash. It only took a few seconds before the car was being pulled into the long stall. The water began hitting the car and the rollers started the loud cleaning cycle.

Gillam grabbed the note pad and began writing quickly. *Check where you can for any hidden bugs in the car.*

Gillam turned on the radio loud and then pointed to the glove box and under the seat as he began feeling around as well. He checked under the dash and console and anywhere he could reach and see, even turning upside down in his seat almost kicking Sam in the head, but coming up empty. Lovett didn't find anything as well and just held up his hands.

They both turned around and checked the back-seat area. Nothing.

As the car was nearing the exit, both Detectives turned around and fastened their seat belts. Gillam turned the radio down.

"That's better," Gillam commented. "Now I can see."

They left the car wash and looked around, but didn't see the black car or van. They drove in silence across the street to their office parking deck. When they parked, Gillam popped the hood and pointed at it for Lovett to check it. Gillam went to the trunk, opened it, and began looking through it. There were lots of hiding places there.

After a few minutes, Lovett came around to the trunk and shook his head indicating that he didn't find anything. Gillam was just about finished when he pulled up a section of the trunk mat covering the left rear wheel well. There he saw something he didn't expect. It was a mobile GPS transmitter. They weren't being bugged. The car was. Wherever it was driven, someone knew right where it was, how long it took to get there, how long it stayed, how many miles it drove, and probably what radio stations were being listened to. There were no markings to show whom it belonged to and Gillam wasn't about to just disconnect it.

After not finding an audio bug, they were a little relieved that their conversations, as far as they could tell, were not being overheard in the car, but that didn't mean other things weren't bugged. Their phones and homes and who knew what else.

Gillam knew the laws about surveillance equipment, wiretaps, and privacy. This was a government vehicle and a GPS unit could be installed legally without their knowledge, *if* it was done by said government. It wasn't their vehicle to do with as they pleased. Gillam and Lovett just borrowed it. But bugging someone else's conversations was a no-no without a court order and you better have a good reason for getting that court order.

The detectives headed up to their office. When they got there, they found Lieutenant Jones was gone as usual. That was a good thing. They both checked their desk, their phones and all around their spaces for any bugs, suspicious items, or things out of place. Nothing appeared out of the ordinary, but they didn't want to take any chances.

Both had several telephone messages waiting for them. Lovett found one from his wife asking about the ballgame next week and the date for Gillam. She stated she tried to call his cell phone, but it was always busy. She called while they were being followed. Bad timing.

Gillam received several messages from Simmons, one from Starling and one from the Chief Medical Examiner. He decided the Chief ME outweighed all the rest right now.

He went to a far end of the office for privacy and for the best reception and called the number on his cell phone not wanting to use the office phone just yet, hoping his cell was safe for now. He got through on the third ring. The Chief Medical Examiner was Dr. Charles Higdon. He had been the Fulton County Medical Examiner for about twenty-three years and was a no-nonsense type of guy. Gillam never pursued any direct contact with him before. Luckily, there had been no need.

When the doctor answered, Gillam identified himself and began by telling him how sorry he was at the loss of Kim.

"Yes, yes, that was tragic," Doctor Higdon agreed. "Now let's get down to cases. Who killed him?"

"Ah, well, I don't know for sure," Gillam stammered at the doctor's direct question. "The department is working on it. I'm sure there will be a full investigation if it's determined it was more than an accident."

"More than an accident?" The doctor repeated. "Son, are you stupid or just incompetent. I got back early this morning and the first thing I did was the autopsy on Doctor Kim. Yes, he was burnt, but not all over. It didn't take me two minutes to see he had been shot in the head. Anyone just looking at the body could see that. The bullet entered the left side of the skull just behind the ear and exited out the right front temple. He died instantly. I got a copy of the accident report and I talked with the Fire-Rescue Unit that got him out of the wagon. Have you talked with them?"

"No sir, not yet. That was going to be one of our next things to do, but I did get a copy of the accident report."

"Did you know Doctor Kim was not driving the wagon when it crashed?"

"What?" Gillam exclaimed. "How on earth could you know that? They needed to use the 'Jaws of Life' to get him out of the wagon. He was alone in the front compartment. The accident report has him listed as the driver. I doubt anyone else was in there."

"Son, I've been doing autopsies since before you were a

squint in your daddy's eye. On the accident report, does it say anything about him wearing a seat belt?"

"Hold on a second." Gillam pulled his copy of the report out of his shirt pocket where he placed it. He unfolded it and looked over the report one more time. "Yes, yes it does. And the air bag deployed as well."

"Well then," Doctor Higdon said, "if Doctor Kim was driving and had an accident that caused that much damage, don't you think there would be some marks left by the seat belt, if he was wearing it, or at least from the air bag when it popped out?"

"But Kim was badly burnt. Surely there wouldn't be any marks visible now."

"Maybe not on the skin's surface," the doctor explained, "but sub-dermal; that's under the skin to you. There were no signs of bruising from belt tension which would have shown from that type of accident, if he was wearing his seat belt and I know he always did. The rescue unit told me they didn't have to cut him out of the seat belt. Yes, the seat belt material was burnt, but the metal clasps were not fastened together. He was not wearing the seatbelt," Doctor Higdon, revealed.

"Also," he continued, "there were no indications the air bag made contact with him in any fashion. You know when those bags come out, they travel pretty fast and they are packed with a fine powder to keep it dry and pliable. When that bag comes out with that much force and that powder, some of it may be injected, to use a layman's term, into the skin, hair, eyes, or nose of the driver. A lot of it would be imbedded into the clothing. It's very likely some of it may even be inhaled if the victim is breathing at the time. The fire may have burnt off trace amounts of the powder if it was present on the outer skin or clothing.

"Chemical tests showed no evidence of any such powder," the doctor said. "There were no indications of any of that powder in him and that tells me he was either dead at the time of the accident and, or not behind the steering wheel of the wagon at the time of the crash, or maybe not even in the wagon altogether. Now, what about that investigation?"

William N. Gilmore

CHAPTER 13

Gillam was speechless. At least for a few seconds. When he regained his composure, he returned to the conversation.

"Doctor Higdon, I need to meet with you to continue this. I don't think now would be a good or safe time to explain what happened while you were gone."

"Safe?" the doctor returned. "What do you mean?"

"Please doctor, I can't go into it right now. There's a lot going on. We need to meet. You may want to have Jaccob there as well."

"Jaccob?' he repeated. What's Jaccob got to do with this?"

"I'll explain the best I can when we meet. Would this afternoon be okay with you?"

"This afternoon? What's wrong with right now? Let's get this thing cleared up as soon as possible. What's the delay?"

"There have been some developments we need to deal with. Trust me; it's for everyone's best interest."

"You better have some answers for me then. I'm not someone you can toy with or play games with. This was a close colleague and friend and I want to know what the hell is going on. Don't make me call your supervisor or the Chief of Police on this. I expect answers and I expect them now."

"Yes sir. I fully understand and I will be happy to tell you all I know when we meet. Just right now, there are things going on that must be dealt with and precautions made. And sir, if you will, please do not discuss any of this with anyone else until we meet. I know this sounds melodramatic, but don't trust anyone and please keep Jaccob close. I think he may be of big help to both of us."

"You may be right that I don't know everything that's going on, son, but let me tell you, I can take care of myself."

"Of that, I have no doubt, sir, but there's no harm in added safety in numbers. We'll be there as soon as we can."

"There you go with that *safe* crap again. Okay, I'll get Jaccob and we'll lock up till you get here, but you better make it snappy, son, or you'll pay holy hell with me and that's one game you don't want to play."

Gillam was reminded of his grandfather who joined the army during the second Great War and his father who served in Korea. Both were tough, get to the point type of guys too. He was glad to have such a strong background. He missed them both.

Next, he called Detective Starling. He relayed what happened so far and asked him to meet with them later at the Medical Examiner's Office. He told him what Doctor Higdon discovered.

"Then I've got a murder on my hands and no suspects or witnesses and now, no crime scene. Can this case get any more screwed up than it already is?"

"I'm just thankful you've only got the one murder so far. We thought earlier that you would have a couple more. Us. And we still don't know who those guys were."

"You're starting to sound like that movie, *Butch Cassidy and the Sundance Kid*. You know, when they were being chased by the posse."

"But we *don't* know who those guys are or what their intentions might be. Are they just following us or trying to trap us? We need someone we can trust that has connections with the Feds who can quietly get some information out of them or if it's *not* the Feds, find out who *is* tailing us and why."

"I'll do what I can. I might be able to check with someone I know. I'll get back to you on that."

"Thanks. I'll call you later and let you know what time to meet us." He also told him he might want to check his car for any hidden electronic devices. He told him why.

Simmons was next on his list and called over to dispatch. He got hold of Simmons and expressed his gratitude for the good work he did on the traffic cameras.

"*Now,* can you tell me what the hell is going on?" Simmons inquired. "Please don't leave me in the dark if I'm going to get my butt chewed out for checking on the FBI or whomever you got issues with."

"I'd tell you, but I don't know myself. Did you get any information at all on those vehicles or where they were headed after we got to the office?"

"I tried to keep an eye on you and them. When you went into the carwash, I lost them. They hightailed it out of the area in different directions and got mixed in with other traffic. I'm afraid when I tried to open the registration site for those particular tags, I was flagged for the intrusion by someone and now *I* might be followed myself, or have a visit from someone in the middle of the night and not wake up in the morning. Just how deep are you guys in this mess?"

"All the way up to our necks, and we're standing on our heads. I'm sorry we got you involved with this, but with your expertise in the electronics over there, we needed someone in a hurry whom we could count on."

"Well, I'm that guy. I'm glad I could help and just remember that next time you want to call me a 'geek'.

"I do need just a little more of your help in a matter. There's a piece of equipment I want you to look at when you get the chance. It's a mobile GPS unit that someone put in our detective car."

"You're kidding me? Someone put a GPS tracker on you guys. Now that takes the cake. How'd you find it?"

"We thought we might have been bugged and started looking in the car for one and I found the GPS unit in the trunk. I thought for sure it would have been under the hood."

"Nah, whoever did it knows what they're doing. If it's put under the hood, there might be some interference from the engine or the electronic components. In the trunk, it has less chance of that. The metal is thinner, so there may or may not be any kind of antenna and it can be connected right to any electrical wiring or it could have a self-contained battery, which I doubt. That would mean they would need to have access to your car anytime to change out a battery or it was just for short term use."

"See, that's what I mean. We need your expertise. I admit you can be a pain in the butt sometimes, but you come through in the clutch. Give me a call when you are about to get off. We have some things to do and we'll get with you later."

"Sure thing. I can't wait. Like I said, just keep me in the loop."

Gillam did believe Simmons was a pain, but sometimes a pain can tell you what ails you and right now there was a heap of ails going around and they needed answers. They were lucky to have someone like Simmons on their team. Simmons would agree.

Lovett received one other message as well. It was from Mr. Granger at the impound lot. He said some rafters found the wrecker. It had been driven into the Chattahoochee River, but not completely submerged. There was no sign of Thompson. He said divers would be going in to see if he was still in the river, but due to the current and visibility, they didn't give it much hope. There was no more to the message.

When Gillam came back to the desk, he told Sam about

his conversations with Doctor Higdon, Starling and Simmons.

"So, Kim was murdered. Surely, it's not the FBI then. I could believe it's the CIA. I think those spooks would kill their mothers if they thought they knew too many secrets. We've got another mystery on our hands now too." He let him listen to Grangers message. Lovett skipped the one from his wife.

"I know you believe in conspiracies, Larry," Lovett said at the end of the recording. "UFO's, the Kennedy assassination, Area 51, all of that. Is that what were up against? Is this some big cover up? People ending up dead, bodies disappearing, people missing. What's next, terrorist attacks on tree houses and lemonade stands, counterfeit Monopoly money, Elvis releasing a new album? It makes about as much sense."

"Don't get out there too far Sam," Gillam said, shaking his head. I may not be able to pull you back. I don't know what to think. I really don't know. We've got to get some help on this. Maybe Starling will come through. Besides each other, we only have a few people we can really trust right now. We need to gather up as much evidence as we can, document everything and make copies of everything just in case, watch our backs and see where it all leads."

"Are you sure you don't want to just head for Montana or Wyoming," Sam said. "We could build our own compound and put up barbed wire and machine-guns. We could hunt bear with bazookas out there."

"Not yet," Larry said, "there's still a lot to do. Plus, I

think I owe it to Kim to find the truth. Somehow, I just know Jones has his hands in all of this. If I could just put it all together and prove he's dirty, I'd give up my pension."

"Wow." Sam exclaimed. "Those are some strong words there my friend. Give up your pension? I'd have a hard time giving Jones the cost of a bullet to the head, but I'd have to do it. We know he's dirty. Catching him is something else. He's protected by some of the big brass and politicos. He's untouchable. I don't know if he's got something on them or what. He's dodged every complaint filed against him and he's buddy-buddy with the Lieutenant over Internal Affairs. Just how do we catch him?"

"I don't know yet," Larry said. "I'm still working on that."

"Work faster," Sam pleaded.

"Bazookas and machine-guns, huh?" Gillam said, questioning Sam's earlier statement and shaking his head again. "And I thought Montana would be the perfect place to retire. Quiet, peaceful, beautiful mountains with fantastic views, good fishing and far away from all of this."

"As far as I'm concerned," Lovett said, "Mars wouldn't be far enough away from this place right now."

William N. Gilmore

CHAPTER 14

Detective Starling did have a few contacts. He made a call on his cell phone to one of those whom he trusted most. In fact, the number he called was a speed dial number he hadn't used in a long time.

"FBI, Special Agent McGill, may I help you?" answered the strong voice with a bit of an Irish brogue which had been Americanized from many years away from home.

"Tommy, this is John Starling. How are you? It's been a little while."

"John. Yes, it's been donkey's years. How's the form? Is everything all right?"

"Oh, I'm fine. I have a couple of friends who could use some help though. Have you got time right now or are you busy with something?"

"No, things are a bit quiet today," Tommy McGill said. "That's a good thing. What have you got on your mind, John? Does it have anything to do with …, eeh, with your old case?"

"No, nothing like that. My friends, a couple of guys here in the Narcotics Squad, believe they're being watched and followed by the FBI or some other government initials. Is there any way of checking on this?"

"Are your friends into something on the gray side or

bumping their noggins with our lads on an investigation?"

"I know these guys. They're straight up. They're good detectives. I don't think it has anything to do with you guys. As far as I know, everything we have so far is local jurisdiction stuff, but there are some irregularities. One of the Fulton County Medical Examiners is dead. At first it looked like an accident, but now were not so sure. Looks like there could be evil afoot."

"I heard about that. What a cryin' shame," Tommy sympathized. "You say it could be a murder, now do you?"

"That's what the Chief ME believes," Starling said. "Plus, there is a body missing from another investigation that was in the wagon at the time of the accident."

"You'd be right then when you said there be irregularities," Tommy acknowledged. "Is the GBI getting their hands into it?"

"I don't know yet," John continued. "No one else knows right now that the accident was probably a murder except just a handful of people. Not even the Police Chief and we're trying to keep it that way for a while until we figure what's going on. There's a big question about whom to trust. I know from everything we've been through ..., well, I'll just say you're one person I know I can count on."

"Thanks for the vote of confidence," Tommy said. "I don't know how much I can help you, but I'll see what I can do. By the way, how's Susan doing?"

"Yeah, I guess it has been a while. We split up about two

years ago. Her idea. She decided she needed to get away from everything that reminded her of those days, which, as it turned out, included me. We tried counseling, support groups, church and even talked about adopting, but everything we did just kept the bad memories alive. She couldn't cope with thinking it was partially her fault, which it wasn't. I thought it would drive her mad. I can't blame her too much, but it was just as bad for me. I don't think she saw that far."

"I'm sorry to hear of that," Tommy said. "It was a mauldy time for all of us. I wish there was something more I could have done."

"You did all you could. There was no way for any of us to know," Starling said with his voice cracking just a little.

Just over five years ago, on a bright Saturday morning, Starlings six-year-old son, Peter, was kidnapped by a deranged child molester and serial killer by the name of Donald Bernard Smith. Peter was outside playing while his mother was inside sewing. There were no screams, no tires squealing, and no witnesses. Peter was just gone. It was only ten o'clock.

John was working in the Larceny Squad at the time. He was at his desk when he got the call. The chilling voice of a man asked him how many pieces of his son he wanted back. Starling didn't believe the man at first. Obviously, it was a crank call. But just the coldness, the cruelty in the voice shook his resolve. Then the man told him about Peter's birthmark and Starling stood up and began to shake.

"Who is this? What do you want?" Starling asked, with anger mixed with concern, still not wanting to believe the voice.

"I just want to play. I needed a new playmate. Peter is such a sweet boy I thought the others would like him too."

"Okay, let me talk to him. Let me see that he's all right. I'll do whatever I need to do to get him back. I just need to tell him it will be all right," Starling pleaded.

"You'll do whatever *I need* you to do," the frightening voice said. "You want your precious Peter back; you'll do just what I say.

"Yes, yes. I'll do whatever you say. Please, let me talk to him. If you really have him, you'll let me—"

The caller abruptly hung up.

Starling immediately called his house and his wife answered.

"Susan, where's Peter? Please tell me Peter's there!"

"John, are you okay? Peter's outside playing. He's been out there all morning," she said, getting up and hurrying to the back door. She opened the door and not seeing Peter right away, she began yelling his name. She ran out to the back yard carrying the phone and continued to call for her son. The swing set and playhouse were empty.

"John, he's not answering!" She started to run around to the front of the house and saw the side gate open. She hoped Peter was around to the front of the house, something he was not allowed to do alone, and forgettingly, left the gate open. Again, she did not see the boy and began looking around franticly up and down the street and yards, yelling his name. There was no sign of Peter.

"Where is he? Do you know where he is?" she asked, sobbing.

"Yes, I think so. I'm on the way home. Don't answer the phone. Don't go out. Lock the doors. I'll have a patrol car there in a few minutes." John didn't wait for an answer from his wife. He was already headed out the door and on the radio calling for a car to get to his residence A.S.A.P. and to secure the area as a crime scene; he would be there in fifteen minutes.

The first car on the scene arrived in less than five minutes and radioed Starling of their arrival and finding his wife home and okay, but shaken.

When Starling got to his house, he found several patrol cars there with his wife crying and talking to one of the officers. She ran up to him and grabbed him. "Where's Peter? Is he hurt? Tell me!" she demanded.

"I think he's all right," he said, not sure if he believed what he was telling her. "Go inside and I'll be right there. I'll tell you what I know. Let me talk with these guys first. Grudgingly she went. Starling walked over and talked with one of the supervisors on the scene. He told him about the call. The supervisor began by calling out the crime scene unit and additional patrol units to check the area. He then made a call to the FBI.

Special Agent Tommy McGill was assigned to the case. He was already on another case involving a child taken from his yard two weeks before in North Georgia. The parents also received taunting calls from an unidentified man. First asking how many pieces of their son did they want back.

No ransom of money was ever asked for even though the mother was a bank official. No threats about calling the police. The man said he 'wanted a playmate'.

The caller only demanded certain things. Things that didn't make since to them. Things they must do if they wanted their precious son back. The father followed the directions of the caller, but declined to call the police at the insistence of his wife fearing reprisals for doing so.

The father, sent on a timed trek for strange items, thought he was trading to get his son back. He was wrong. Very wrong. The father finally called the police in a panic after receiving another call, this time telling him where to find a box. The contents of the box was a bloody piece of the young victim.

When the FBI received that case, a small task force worked on it attempting to locate the boy and identify the man by checking any enemies of the parents, especially the father, a Probation Officer.

They checked for sex offenders, child molesters, ex-cons, and even homeless people. They checked for similar cases in other jurisdictions and states and found a disturbing pattern which included at least four other kids of similar ages taken over several weeks in Kentucky, South Carolina and Tennessee.

The missing kid's parents included a school principal, a city councilman, a newspaper reporter, and an attorney. Two of those kids were found, but tragically, not alive after exhaustive searches and partial clues left by an unidentified suspect. The other two have not been found.

The small task force grew into an army. The agents were able to backtrack the information and came up with a short list of possible suspects. On that list was a recently released child molester named Donald Bernard Smith. Smith served seven years of a ten-year sentence in Kentucky.

He fit the profile perfectly; a loner, abused as a child, minor run-ins with the law as a juvenile, an underachiever, and a school dropout. He enjoyed torturing small animals, drawing sadistic pictures of torture and death in notebooks, and was known to have experimented with LSD and other drugs.

He was now 28 years old, no family left to speak of and no place to go. He was full of hate for authority figures. The only reason he was released from prison was due to the overcrowded conditions, his age, and he never caused any trouble while there.

He was quiet; a loner; not a part of any gang or uprising. Fellow inmates thought him weird and peculiar, or maybe just insane. They may have been right on all counts. Now he was out, and the trouble really began.

Special Agent McGill met with the Starlings at their home. John remembered that day too well. It haunted him every day, every night. It was something you never want to happen to anyone and something you never expect to happen to you.

"Do any of these photos look like anyone you might have seen recently or that you may have arrested in the past?" McGill said, showing him several pictures including one of Smith.

"No," Starling said, throwing the pictures back down on a table, "but I swear I'll find this guy and get my boy back and make sure the sick bastard never gets a chance to hurt anyone ever again. No matter what it takes."

There was no note, no witness, and no physical evidence of any kind on the scene. Not even any kind of report of suspicious people or vehicles in the neighborhood. Every mailman, deliveryman, neighbor, lawn care person, and salesman was checked and double-checked. All video cameras in the area were checked, but with negative results.

Another call was received several hours later, but this time to the Starlings residence. John took the call as the FBI listened in and recorded the same male voice John recognized from the earlier call.

"I know you got the FBI there, so I'll be brief. Take a bus to the CNN Center, get off and go west on Marietta Street for five blocks; take a right into the ally and look under the dumpster there. Take a backpack with these items and these items only. No nasty guns now. One pound of sugar; one pack of Pall Mall unfiltered cigarettes; one peppermint candy cane; one box of raspberry Jell-O, and your cell phone. Don't worry, I've got the number. Oh, and come alone and no transmitters. You have one hour starting …, now. I'm watching. If you screw up, he's dead."

"Let me speak to my son," John begged, "just to let me know he's still alive."

"Times going by pretty fast. If you want to waste time, go ahead. If you're not there in fifty-nine minutes and fifty seconds with the things on my list, I'll cut his pretty little head off. Are you still there? See you soon."

"No!" screamed Starling. The line was dead. Susan was sobbing again. "Oh, my God. How can I get there in time? What was all that that he wanted and why?"

One of the FBI agents wrote down the list of items and relayed them to another over the phone. Another agent who was monitoring the call told McGill the call was being made on an unlisted cell phone, possibly a disposable one. They would try to see if they could get a tower fix for at least a general area.

"He's playing a sick game with us. Okay, here's what we do now," McGill said, quickly formulating a plan. "First, they might not mean a thing, but we get the items on that bloody list. John, do you have a backpack here? Never mind, we'll get you one. Get the Commissioner of Transportation on the phone and get the bus line schedule and routes for the CNN Center stop," he said to an agent already typing on a laptop.

"We'll have one of our lads get on board at one of the

stops with the backpack and hand it off to you with the items. I want coverage of the area now," he told another agent. "But don't stand out like FBI agents, look like regular blokes, if that's at all possible. We have no time to set up regular surveillance and this guy may already be on the scene or miles away. This may just be the first stop and we may get directed to other locations. I want several other units mobile, but blocks away."

McGill knew in his heart it didn't matter if John was on time or not. He didn't want to believe what he already knew. He also didn't want to tell him how the other two kids looked when they were found. They needed to do something, so for now they played the sick game of this lunatic while his team used what they knew to try and locate him.

John still wore his ankle holster which held the Smith and Wesson, model-37. A reliable, five-shot, air-weight revolver. It wasn't noticeable under his pant leg. He left his other sidearm on the dresser. He headed back downstairs and kissed his wife. He didn't know if this would be the last time he would ever see her, but he felt the need to try and reassure her that things would be alright; at least for the moment.

"We'll get him back," John said, holding his wife, looking into her tear-filled, hopeful eyes. "Everything will be okay. I'll see you soon and I'll have Peter with me. I promise," he said, hoping every word was true, but fearing she didn't believe it either.

"Okay, Tommy, I'm headed to the bus stop up the street,"

John stated on his cell phone. "How do we know it will be on time and not make any extra stops along the way to delay me?"

"Because we have one of our lads on the way with a bus that he is driving. It will only have one passenger, which would be you, and he knows where to pick up our agent with the backpack. There's a car about a half mile ahead to radio any problems along the way."

"You guys are fast. And what about those items? Some of those are hard to come by these days. Is there time to get them?"

"We have our resources. Come on, let's go. We only have about a half hour left."

"Thirty-two minutes," John said, keeping a close eye on the time.

William N. Gilmore

CHAPTER 15

Starling just reached the bus stop when a city bus with a 'CNN Center' digital placard stopped, opened its doors, and the driver told him to get in. Starling got on the bus and discovered he indeed was the only passenger.

"Sit down," the driver instructed him. "We need to get through this traffic, pick up the other agent, and get you dropped off in less than fifteen minutes so you can make the trip to that alley in time. My name's Carrington. You can call me George. We've been fully briefed. The other agent is still in route to his pick-up point and should be there about the time we are. There was a little trouble finding one of the items, but we have them all now. We should be there in about seven minutes."

George was wearing a voice transmitter in his ear so everyone on the teams knew in real time what was happening as he spoke it.

The ride seemed to take forever with George calling out the location every couple of seconds.

John's cell phone rang. The display only indicated 'Incoming call' and he answered.

"You don't have much time left," the voice taunted. Did you and your friends get everything? Are they with you now?"

"We're working on it. No, I'm on the bus and on the way.

I'll be there on time. I'd like to talk to Peter now, please," John said, using a politer tactic he hoped would work.

"Peter can't come to the phone right now, he's a little tied up," the man laughed loudly at his own stupid joke. "You just make sure you get there on time and with everything I want. No tricks, and no cops, except you of course." More laughing. "And don't forget, I'll be watching."

"Why are you doing this?" John pleaded.

"Because I can. Isn't this fun?" He hung up.

The bus slowed and stopped beside a building. A man dressed in ragged blue jeans, with an open button down shirt over a blue tee shirt got on. He was carrying a large shopping bag.

Once on the bus, he sat behind John and told him his name was Evans and he had a backpack with the items in it. He slid the bag up beside Starling and he took it out of the bag. He opened it and made sure himself the items were there. They were. Every one of them. He adjusted the straps and put the backpack on. Evans then went to the back of the bus.

George said that they were coming up on the CNN Center in about twenty seconds. John got ready and as soon as the bus stopped, he got off and headed towards the alley as instructed. George let all the teams know Starling was on foot now as the bus continued.

One of the FBI teams had Starling in sight and watched as he walked the few blocks to the alley. They didn't see anyone following him. They had the alley under surveillance not long after the call was received with the instructions. John had four minutes left. Plenty of time.

Starling's phone rang again. He answered it and the awful voice was there again.

"You're close, very close. You were right, you'll make it on time. Now, you're sure you have all the items I wanted?"

"Yes, I have them. I'm just about a minute away."

"You have the pack of unfiltered Pall Mall cigarettes?"

"Yes."

"You have the Raspberry Jell-O?"

"Yes."

"You have the peppermint candy cane?"

"Yes," John said, getting tired of the game he was being forced to play.

"You have the pound of brown sugar?"

"Ye ...; what? You didn't say *brown* sugar," John said panicky. "You just said a pound of sugar!"

"You should have asked," he snickered. "You still have almost three minutes. I suggest you find a pound of brown sugar mighty quick. You want Peter. I want my brown sugar. Maybe your FBI friends can help. I tell you what. I'll give you a full five minutes. Starting from right now. There, you see. I'm a reasonable guy. I'll call back soon. Very, very, soon."

There were no grocery stores in the area. John called McGill on his cell and told him what happened. McGill already put out a radio call to anyone near any store to get a pound of brown sugar and call in when they found it. McGill overheard the conversation John was having with the bug planted in the backpack.

McGill got several calls almost right away. Every agent who went into a store within a few miles of the location told him the same thing. Every store was sold out of brown sugar. Someone came in and bought every box, every bag of brown sugar in all the stores earlier that day and there was not any in stock.

Time was up.

Starling was at the alley, but he was missing one of the items. Now he waited for the next terrifying call from the kidnapper. Dreading it to come; hoping it wouldn't.

Starling still went into the alley and over to the only dumpster which was there. He dropped the backpack on the ground and looked under the dumpster as earlier instructed and he saw a small white box. He grasped the box; a red ribbon tied around it and 'To John' written on the outside. He untied the ribbon, slowly lifted the top open, and found inside a layer of cotton. He lifted the cotton and what he saw made him gasp.

He sat down right there and began sobbing. In the box was a small finger with dried blood around it. It had been removed from its owner with a not-so-sharp instrument. Under the finger was a folded piece of paper, also with dried blood on it. Leaving the finger in the box, he removed the paper and unfolded it. The note read:

This is to prove I do have Peter. How many more pieces of Peter do you want back?

Again, John's phone rang. This time he wasn't so polite. He answered it saying, "You sick bastard! What have you done? Why would you do such a hideous thing? How could you hurt a child like that?" Starling was crying, wondering what other dreadful things may have been done to Peter.

"Did you like your present? Would you like some more? I have some bigger boxes."

"Stop this! Is Peter still alive? Just tell me!"

"This has been such a fun game. Thanks for playing. I almost hate to end it, but I have places to be and things to do. Other playmates are waiting."

"Wait! Where's my son?"

There was no answer. There never would be.

He failed. Not relying on the fact that he was tricked by some demented, sick S.O.B., but that he let his son down. It was his fault. He also promised his wife he would bring him home safe. He sat there sobbing.

McGill ordered the FBI teams moved in and after checking out the surrounding area for suspects, booby traps and other immediate concerns, they cordoned off the area as a crime scene. The box with the finger was taken from John. At first, he didn't want to give it up. But he eventually knew it needed to be sent to the crime lab for testing to verify it was Peter's finger.

There was little doubt in anyone's mind.

McGill walked up beside John and sat down next to him. He let him cry for a while and then said to him, "I'm sorry, John. This isn't over. We have some good info the rest of the team has worked up. We have an area we believe the calls were being made from. There's a cell tower not far from here where most of the calls were being routed through. The times match up and we've got a number. It matches the calls from earlier today at your house and your office.

Starling just looked at McGill without speaking.

"I have several of our lads checking videos at the stores where all the brown sugar was bought up and several others checking them within a mile of where the cell tower is located. I'm sure we'll have something soon."

John still didn't say anything. He just kept looking at Tommy.

He's in shock, Tommy thought. *I would be too.*

"He's gone. Our Peter's gone," he finally said.

"We don't know that. You can't just give up. You must keep up hope." McGill wished he had a little hope left too.

Just then, McGill's phone rang and he saw it was one of his agents. Upon answering it, he got up, walked off a short distance, and got into a hurried conversation. He ended that call and he quickly made another. He spoke for a minute or two and ended that call.

He walked back over to John and told him one of the

stores where the brown sugar was purchased possessed a video of a man in a hood and sunglasses making the purchase and a clerk identified the picture of Donald Bernard Smith as the man making the purchase.

"I notified the other teams and they are showing the picture of Smith around the area now. I'm headed over there. Want a lift?" He reached down offering his hand. John looked up for a few seconds.

"You bet I do." He grabbed Tommy's hand and was pulled to his feet.

William N. Gilmore

CHAPTER 16

McGill headed for the area with Starling as his passenger. John asked to see the picture of Smith again. He stared at the picture a long time. Long enough for McGill to have driven to the area and meet with his agents. More good news. One of the liquor stores in the area identified the picture of Smith as a frequent new customer.

"He's staying in the area," Tommy said. Speaking into his radio he barked out orders, "Have all units available converge on this area and cordon off a five-block area. I want surveillance and teams to go door to door showing his picture."

McGill and Starling went to one of the convenience stores in the area and went in. McGill showed his badge along with the picture of Smith to the clerk through his security glass. The clerk looked at the picture for a minute and said he thought the guy was one who came in a few times lately. He thought the guy may live around the corner.

McGill began walking out the door, talking with John behind him when a guy tried to walk in. Tommy looked around and his eyes went wide like a deer in headlights. Smith acted first and hit McGill squarely in the jaw. Tommy hit the floor in a heap. Smith began running and John, trying to get around McGill tripped a second, but got his footing in time to stay within ten to twelve feet behind.

Smith, younger and in better shape, ran like the mad man he was, but John was on a mission. Smith jumped over fences, and ditches, but Starling stayed right with him. In fact, he seemed to be catching up. People were watching, pointing, getting out of the way of the two. John almost grabbed Smith once, but he dodged him at the last second and they both went wide of a building going around the corner.

Smith was running up a sidewalk along some buildings when a car tried to cut him off by pulling over the curb. The car was driven by McGill. Smith went over the front of the car just in time and John was forced to run behind it giving Smith a little more lead. As they ran, McGill could hear sirens of police cars coming into the area. The perimeter was being reset to keep Smith bottled in. He wasn't getting away.

Smith cut down an alley cars couldn't get through easily and ran for some steps. He went for a door at the top of those steps, but it didn't open. He jumped over a railing and continued to run, but his lead shrunk. He turned down a smaller alley and again Starling was right behind him. Starling again tried to make a stab at Smith and he was just able to grab his shirt before they both went spilling on the ground. Smith got up and started to run again, but saw the alley was a dead end.

Starling was between him and the way back out. Smith stopped, looked around and saw a large pipe on the ground. He picked it up and started towards Starling, just as he was sitting up, sucking air. Starling ducked as the pipe was swung where his head had been just a fraction of a second before.

"So, you want to join your boy?" Smith said, gasping for breath himself. "I haven't taken on anyone your size in a while."

"You killed my son, you bastard," John said, trying to get up.

"Oh, I did more than that. You should have heard him scream for mommy and daddy. But they didn't come." He swung the pipe again, this time hitting Starling on the left arm, knocking him down again, but missed on the down swing when John rolled away.

Starling barely got to one knee. His left arm was useless now, probably broken. Smith was only a few feet away, breathing heavy and holding the pipe with both hands. He had a smile on his face; an evil, sadistic smile. John knew Smith was about to make the final blow with the deadly pipe.

Starling looked Smith right in the eyes and said, "I made a couple of promises today. I'll never live down the ones I couldn't keep, but by God, I'll keep the one I can."

Smith started towards John with the pipe raised above his head and Starling having pulled the revolver from the hidden ankle holster pushed it out in front of him and fired. Smith recoiled back a few steps and dropped the pipe. The smile on his face changed to a grimace. He looked down and saw the widening red spot on his chest. He stood there for a second and he heard the two other shots, but never felt them. He fell into a knelling position and slumped over with his face hitting the ground. He didn't feel that either.

McGill came around the corner of the alley just in time to see Smith falling on his face and John on one knee with a revolver in one hand, his left arm hanging limp by his side. He went over to Smith and checked him to verify he was dead. He was.

Tommy holstered his own weapon and he turned to check on John just in time to see him put the revolver under his chin. Tommy never moved so fast. He tackled Starling at the same time he pushed the gun away. Being so close, the gunshot was deafening.

Tommy was almost too scared to look up, but when he did, John was on the ground in a ball, sobbing. The shot missed both of them, thank God; the revolver falling a safe distance from Starling. He didn't want him to have a second chance. He went over, picked up the revolver, and put it in his pocket. He let John lie there.

The ringing in his ears was so loud that when he tried to radio his other agents he couldn't hear any response. He told them they needed an ambulance and a crime scene unit at his location and there was one officer hurt and one suspect down. Down for good.

In a very short time, several agents appeared in the alley and met with McGill. John was able to sit up holding his left arm. An ambulance arrived, parked on the street and the EMT's hurried into the alley. They were about to go to Smith first and McGill told them to forget the bastard and treat Starling.

The ringing was still there, but McGill could hear if someone was close enough and spoke loud enough. One of his agents told him they were checking the area and found a stolen van around the corner near an abandoned building. They said the van was empty, but they hadn't checked the building yet. It was locked up and they were waiting on further orders.

The EMT's were putting Starling on a gurney. Through his own ringing ears, he barely overheard the agents speaking in a loud voice to McGill.

"I'm going with you," Starling said, trying to swing up to a sitting position on the gurney while holding his bad arm.

"Oh, no you don't," one of the EMT's said. "You can't go anywhere except with us to the hospital. Your left arm is broken and it could be a compound fracture. If you move around too much you could cause it to poke out, or even cut a vein or an artery. You're ours for now," he said pushing Starling back down on the gurney, but meeting some resistance.

"I have to go. I need to see for myself," he was saying loudly as McGill walked over.

McGill could make out the words by reading John's lips and expression. He already knew what John was going to say anyway. That was the easy part.

"Maybe it's best you don't," the agent said. "I don't know what we'll find, if anything. Let us do our job now and I'll let you know something as soon as I can. I'll take care of things for you. Don't worry about that."

CHAPTER 17

The ambulance with Starling was finally in route to the hospital with a police escort. A patrol car would take his wife to the hospital to be with him. Nothing was to be said to her about what was found. Nothing.

The ME's wagon arrived. The new Assistant Medical Examiner, George Kim and one of his assistants waited to take the body of Donald Bernard Smith. McGill asked them to stand by due to what they may find in another potential crime scene related to the case.

An FBI entry team arrived and after getting fully dressed out in their raid gear, a go ahead was received to make the entry into the building after a search warrant was issued by a federal judge. The order was given over the phone to expedite the process.

The entry team breached the main entrance while other doors were guarded. They met no resistance going in, finding no booby traps. The only job for the entry team was to clear the building of any potential suspects, make the building safe for the other agents, and to secure the area while the investigation proceeded. The entry team did their job. How they were able to do their job was the question. Clearing the building, they saw things that turned their stomach; things that made them cry;

things that no person should ever see.

"Sweet Jaysus!" Special Agent Tommy McGill said, as he entered the building, crossed himself, and said a silent prayer. The entry team did not find a living soul in the building, but what they did find would come to be called *The Devil's Workshop* in newspapers, newsrooms, and tabloids around the globe.

The missing victims of Donald Bernard Smith were found. McGill possessed pictures of both victims along with physical and clothing descriptions. He made the preliminary identification of both victims from what was left of them in the building. He was pretty sure anyway. The M.E. would be able to tell him more. He turned the scene over to the crime scene techs and the M.E. He went back out to his car, got in, sat there and cried. He cried for the victims, for their parents, and he cried believing somehow, he had failed to protect them.

McGill still needed to tell John and his wife about Peter. He promised him. And although he believed that John knew, his wife was still holding out hope. He would be the one to dash that hope. He would forever be the one who delivered the news that their only son, who was stolen away, terrible, inhuman things done to him, was killed at the hands of a stranger. Not for revenge, not in anger, but just for fun. How do you tell someone that there are people in this world who kill children for fun and expect them to understand; to live their lives in some normal fashion after that fact; to remain sane; and to somehow still believe in a benevolent God?

After several minutes, Tommy started up the car and began the drive to the hospital. It was the longest drive of his life. When he arrived, he found Starling already in a room and his wife with him.

He talked with the attending doctor first and found John's left arm was indeed broken, but that it appeared to be a simple break with no other serious internal damage. The doctor wondered about the gunpowder burns on the left side of John's face. They were treated and bandaged as well. He was under a mild sedative. McGill also explained to the doctor that his wife may need a sedative as well after she received the news about their son. He understood and ordered the nurse to prepare one just in case.

McGill took a deep breath and entered the room. Susan stood up, wide-eyed and scared to ask the question. John looked at Tommy and his worst fears were confirmed. Susan fell back into the chair and began sobbing.

"I'm so sorry," Tommy said.

☞

The funeral for Peter Starling was a somber event. It was a cloudy morning almost a week after receiving that dreadful call. There was not an open casket viewing at the funeral home. There couldn't be.

A police escort moved the procession quickly through the traffic. Relatives, friends, and even complete strangers crowded the cemetery. Peter would be buried next to his paternal grandparents.

John, his left arm in a cast, supported in a sling, wore a black jacket draped over his shoulders. No longer needed, the bandage on his face had been removed. Signs of scorched skin and redness were still visible. Susan, in a black dress and black hat with a veil, sat nearest the casket. She refused to talk with anyone, including John, and cried the entire time.

Flower arrangements were everywhere; from everywhere. The service was almost too long; too many words about death and life, life after death, and the innocence of youth. John almost told the preacher to get it over with already. Dragging it out seemed cruel.

Tommy McGill stood over to a side away from everyone. He hadn't talked with Starling since that night at the hospital. There was nothing else to say and little to discuss until both were ready.

The service concluded, but Susan didn't want to leave. People came up to the couple to express their sympathy and Susan hardly acknowledged them. Some began to disperse slowly, some shaking hands, others still weeping.

One little boy who went to pre-school with Peter slowly walked up to Susan and gave her a coloring he drew of Peter in Heaven. Susan hugged him and thanked him. It was the only reaction other than crying she had shown that day. When the little boy was gone, she hugged the paper. After several minutes, she got up and headed back to the limousine which brought them to the cemetery. She didn't wait for John. She got in and sat there hugging the picture.

John spotted McGill and walked over to him.

"Hello Tommy, thank you for coming. Is there any news yet?"

"I've been waiting to finish my report until the Medical Examiner concluded his investigation. He still needs your statement, but that should be all of it. I told him I would talk with you. He understands you need some time, but there are some things we need to talk about first. I know now isn't the best time and I see Susan may be ready to go. We can meet anytime, or if you want, you can just call and I'll arrange for you to meet with one of my other lads at the office."

"Tommy, whatever you may think, I don't blame you. You did what you could. And you don't need to worry about me. I acted on a selfish impulse during a moment of weakness and that won't ever happen again."

"That's good, but after all this is over, if you ever need to talk or just get away, ring me up. I have a cabin on a lake. There's really good fishing, better yet, solitude."

"I just might take you up on that one day. How about I call you tomorrow and we can get it over with. I think it's best I get Susan home for now."

"Sure. Give her my best." He wasn't sure what else to say. He went home and got himself right scuttered.

William N. Gilmore

CHAPTER 18

The next morning John called Tommy as promised and agreed to meet with him at his office to give him the statement and to find out where the Medical Examiner's investigation stood.

When John entered the FBI office he was envious of the space and cleanliness and how well things appeared to be organized. Something the Atlanta Police Department should think about. He was escorted to the office of Special Agent in Charge, Tommy McGill.

Tommy met him at his office door, showing him in and told him to have a seat. John couldn't help but notice the photos along with plaques and trophies on the walls and bookcases. There were photos of Tommy and Presidents, Tommy and the Pope, Tommy and–Tommy?

"That be my twin brother," he said, noticing Starling staring at the picture. "He's a Police Inspector in Dublin. He decided to stay in Ireland when I came to the States and became a citizen here. That was just over twenty years ago, now. It was a bit of a bittersweet decision. For both of us. But we talk almost every week and I've been back several times. He's been here once and doesn't like it and swears he's the one who made the better decision."

"And what do you think?"

"I think we both made the right decision."

John also noticed a large evidence envelope on Tommy's desk. He was almost afraid of what it contained. Things used by Smith to hurt Peter; pictures of Peter's mutilated body, or even worse. He slowly sat in a chair across the desk from Tommy.

Tommy sat at his desk. He looked at John for a second and took a deep breath. "The ME's report states that Peter's death occurred between eight o'clock and ten o'clock a.m. and his finger was removed sometime afterwards. He was gone before you got the first call, John. The other boys had been dead about twenty-four to thirty hours. There was nothing more you could have done."

John felt like he wanted to cry again, but in some strange way, he was relieved; relieved his son didn't suffer prolonged pain and hurt; relieved that he knew what happened to his son unlike some of the parents of the other kidnapped children; relieved in knowing that the sick bastard would never hurt anyone ever again.

"We found that most probably, ether was used in his taking. We found a bottle in the stolen van along with a cloth with traces of ether on it. There was a small stuffed dog and other stuffed animals in the van along with duct tape. In the building, we found a map with your house; office; CNN Center; and the alley where the finger was found; circled. He knew all your telephone numbers as well. One other thing; we found another map with circles. He was planning to take another child from this area. He's been identified as the son of a television station owner."

Tommy opened the evidence envelope. John held his breath for a moment, almost wanting to close his eyes. From it, Tommy pulled John's revolver and a small bag containing the remaining unfired bullet.

"I got permission to return your gun. Ballistics tests were conducted, as is procedure and, of course, there's no problem."

There were four spent shells and one live shell left. Three slugs were recovered from Smith and another was found fragmented in the alley after hitting the side of a building. That was the one which was fired when Smith jumped you."

"What are you saying, Tommy?" Starling said, cocking his head.

"The two of you fought over the gun and it went off next to your face. It dazed you for a second, but you were able to get away from him. He picked up an iron bar and came after you while you were down. He hit you in the left arm and broke it. He came at you again with the bar and that's when you were forced to shoot him."

"Tommy?"

"Just as I was coming around the corner I saw him standing over you with the bar about to hit you again and you didn't have a choice."

Starling just stared at Tommy for what seemed like minutes.

"That's the way it happened, right?"

Starling didn't answer.

Right?" Tommy repeated, no longer so much of a question.

"Yeah,' John said, lowering his head, "that's the way it happened."

Starling wrote out his statement. It was the first time he ever put something in a sworn statement which wasn't true. If he put what really happened in the alley he would be forced to undergo massive psychological evaluations; something he was sure would be required with the tragic murder of his son and the shooting death of a suspect.

Moreover, he would possibly be put on a suicide watch, suspended, or given a medical discharge from the force; none of which he wanted. Now he focused on a new mission in the police department. He wanted to get those types of people off the street. He figured the best place to start would be to put in for the Homicide Squad. It might be hard for a while, but work would be the best thing to keep his mind occupied with something other than the events of the past week. A week which would last a lifetime.

He finished the statement and with a heavy sigh, signed it. He looked down at it; words on a piece of paper, too many lives gone, others destroyed. How many more lives did this monster have control over during his rampage? How much pain would he still generate from the grave? At least it wouldn't be physical pain directed at children.

McGill took the paper and John didn't even look up for a minute. Tommy signed it as well before putting it in a thick folder. "I'll get a copy over to the Medical Examiner's office. That should conclude his investigation."

John and Tommy agreed to get together for drinks or dinner sometime. Or maybe even a fishing trip to that cabin by the lake. They shook hands and Tommy watched him leave hoping he would be all right. He hoped *he* would be all right. He decided to call his brother in Ireland.

Just as he was about to dial the phone, an agent knocked on his door. Tommy waved him in.

"Yes"

"Sorry sir," the agent said. "I just wanted to see what you wanted us to do with all the brown sugar we found in that building?"

The FBI would work on the Donald Bernard Smith case for years, studies would be made, books written, and even a documentary filmed. Neither John nor Tommy assisted in any of the ventures. They both refused interviews, book and movie deals, even speculations on the case. Sometimes, bad memories needed to die too. Too often, they run a lifetime and refused to die, even of old age.

William N. Gilmore

CHAPTER 19

After getting the information from Starling on the car and the van, Tommy McGill started making some inquiries. He first checked the registration and found the block was there as reported. No big deal; usual tactics when working undercover, there were back doors to that. He made some calls. He got in touch with one of his former computer forensic guys, Azira Hazar. The FBI computer techs and IT people were good, but Azira was a master on computers and he was on the outside now.

He worked for the FBI for a while after graduating from MIT, but resigned after it was learned he infiltrated several casino's computers in Las Vegas and managed to acquire a fortune in comps and airline miles using the Bureau's computers. He might not have been caught if he hadn't been having so much fun and watched more closely how much he was massing.

He set off a bunch of alerts. He couldn't use the casino comps anyway. He was only nineteen and underage to gamble, not to mention he was afraid to fly. The casinos were not amused, only declining to prosecute for an exchange of some unique, state-of-the-art technology programing Azira came up with which could be used in their surveillance security. The deal was secretly brokered by McGill.

Azira, now working from home with his own computer

set up, contracted with computer software companies writing programs for sophisticated computer games making three times what the FBI paid him. One of the casinos offered him a job when he turned twenty-one making even more.

Tommy made the call to Azira and asked if he faced any real challenges lately. Azira admitted all he was into was the hacking into NASA radio transmissions and talking with the astronauts on the ISS, the International Space Station. NASA never reported the breach and refused to release the audio tapes. This caused a report of a cover-up about the astronauts in contact with aliens.

"Azira, how would you like to help me out with a computer problem?"

"What's wrong, you're hardware now your software?" He laughed. "Having a problem with your floppy?" he continued the banter.

"Don't be a muppet. I have a blocked site I need access to which may have some nawful government entity behind it. Something which may be right up your alley. Possible conspiracy, black ops, *Men in Black,* type of stuff."

Azira smiled. "You're kidding, right? You're really calling because your hard drive crashed or you forgot your password."

"No. It's the real yoke this time. I need your help to crack the block on this site. I need it to be discreet. No trace left behind. Are you up for it?"

"Usual price?"

"If you can have it by this afternoon, I'll make it double."

"Okay, two it is. You can give me the info over the phone, it's safe."

"You have a filter on your phone, I'm sure. Always the careful one."

Azira got busy writing a program which would allow him to enter the site, hopefully without detection, but if he was detected it would provide so many junctions and routings which anyone attempting to trace it back would be busy for months if not forever.

When he was ready, he hooked up several computers for recording and storing information when he entered the site. He entered the registration site and put in the information for the car and the van. Information blocked. Obviously, some kind of government intervention.

When he tried to get past the block, he was detoured to another site, then another, and still another. Azira possessed some tricks; unknown to the public, type tricks, to try. He got into one of the backdoors and found he was being routed to all kinds of different places. Azira began typing as fast as he could, starting some programs, changing others, routing information, and doing everything within his grasp just to stay ahead of firewalls, security software, and other programs.

Azira couldn't remember ever being so challenged just

trying to access a site. His fingers flew, his mind whirled, and he thought his computers would start smoking at any time. At last, he made some progress and got directed to a main site; it looked military, that's as far as he went, they were good. Someone on the other side decided not to try to beat him at his own game and just shut the system down from their side. His screen went blank. They knew they were being hacked, but he hoped his own protection was working. He recorded all the information he received so far, which really wasn't much. He brought up the picture of the main title page of the site.

Operation Back Street

In cooperation with:

United States Department of Defense

United States Department of Homeland Security

United States Justice Department

Centers for Disease Control

"Rutt row. Now what have I gotten into," he said. Then he thought, *This is going to cost Tommy a whole lot more.* He got back on his computer and tried to find any information on *Operation Back Street,* but it came back a blank except for a gay porno. Not interested.

He opened the web sites of all the departments listed. He checked *Operation Back Street* on each site, but came up empty. He wondered why the CDC was listed with the others. He thought McGill could come up with something since it involved the DoJ and Homeland Security; the FBI's stepbrothers. Well, part of a dysfunctional family anyway.

He called Tommy and got him at his office. He gave him the bad news about not finding out about the car and the van, but told him about what he did find.

"*Operation Back Street.* I've never heard of any such yoke. Must be some black bag funded operation. I'll check it out. Thanks, Azira. I know I owe you big, so we'll go ahead and make it a case."

"My thoughts exactly. You're a good man, Tommy McGill."

"Just pull up your knickers and keep trying to see if there's anything more which can help me find out what this *Operation Back Street* is and who's running it."

"Okay. You were right about this being a challenge. Whoever does their computer security is good. Very good. I see this as a cat and mouse game. I'm the mouse going after the cheese and they're the cat trying to catch and eat me. They've put up walls and barriers to keep me from the cheese. They may have traps and dead ends waiting for me, but I'm going to beat them and then I'll find out who I beat and rub it in their face."

"Eh ..., did I mention discreet?" Tommy asked. "I'd like to find out about these guys, not the other bloody way around. I'm not trying to make a name for myself. I'm trying to keep it quiet. Can it be done?"

"Yeah, sure. You take the fun out of everything. I'll keep

checking and I'll be in touch if anything pops up. I still have a few tricks up my sleeve. That's why I'm called, *The Magician*," he said, sitting up a little straighter and smiling.

Azira did have a few tricks. Some he couldn't tell Tommy about. Tricks which could get him prison terms of ten to twenty years if caught. He learned his lesson before; now, he just wouldn't get caught.

CHAPTER 20

The young girl saw the warning on her computer screen of an unauthorized entry attempt into their mainframe. She repulsed a few in the past, mainly low-level inquiries, but they appeared to becoming more and more frequent. This time though was different. She could tell someone was using sophisticated equipment and techniques. This was no amateur. This was someone who knew what they were doing. *Well, so do I*, she thought to herself. *Bring it on.*

There were firewalls and security systems built into the computer mainframe, and then there was her. She was the ultimate security for the whole electronic *Pandora's Box*.

No one, not even the general himself, could get into the system unless she wanted them to. Now someone was trying to get by her and she wasn't going to have it. She began typing, setting up some more of her pre-arranged blocks and dead end routings while also setting into motion a backtrack system to see just who this hacker was.

She underestimated him. He was good; better than she ever encountered, and he was fast. Somehow, he got past her for just a second and realizing it, she shut the system down to stop the intrusion.

Doing so, she also shut down the ongoing trace on the

hacker. She was nervous, concerned about what she should say to her superiors. She was absolutely sure no vital information got out, and she was sure she could block the hacker if he should ever try again. She was positive he would try again. Someone that good made a name for himself somewhere. She didn't know if it was a government agency, a private company, someone with their own agenda, or someone who just got lucky.

Within the computer-geek, black-hat community, there were those who became known because of certain unauthorized sites they got into, viruses they created, games they made or played, or other havoc they caused.

Some were known only by nickname and some by prison number. Some were ghosts who never let you know who they were. At one time or another, she was all the above, but now, she needed to play the ghost, or she felt she would become one for real. These guys here didn't play games. She didn't want to see just how far they would go.

She got on the phone, "This is Jenny, let me speak to the general."

"General Cunningham," the voice itself demanding respect.

"General, it's Jenny. There's been another attempt to enter the mainframe."

"All right. Usual precautions in place? No breach? Right?"

There was too long of a pause in her response and the

general knew that meant trouble.

"Tell me there was no breach, Miss. Jordan."

"There was no real breach, General. Someone attempted to hack into the system from an unknown location. They got access for just a second and I shut it down before they could maneuver anywhere. I know they had no way to access any information. All other systems are secure and show no unauthorized entry. To be safe, I've set up additional firewalls, changed access codes, and put additional safeguards on the entire system."

"Safeguards? You tell me some snot-nosed kid with a game console, or on his daddy's laptop accidentally opened one of the most top secret computer sites in the world and you are telling me you have safeguards?"

"Yes sir, but I don't think it was a kid and I don't think it was an accident. Someone was able to bypass the security in place and if I hadn't been able to delay them and then shut the system down, they may have gained access to possible sensitive material."

"Do you know who the hacker is or where they are operating?"

"Not yet, but I'm working on it."

"How long before you have it?"

"General, I can't just pull it out of a hat. I don't know if I ever will. Maybe if he tries again and I'm ready for him, then maybe I can trace it back to him. Whoever this hacker is, he's damn good. He covers his tracks very well. He's as good as anyone I've ever come across."

"You let me know right away if there are any more attempts and you make sure no one can get into our mainframe. You hear?"

Although Jenny wasn't in the military, she wanted to come to attention and salute when she answered, "Yes Sir." Instead, she just hung up the phone, giving a big sigh. She was in too deep now. They would never let her off the hook. She didn't see any way out.

Jenny Jordan had been made an offer. Like the saying in the movie it came from, it was an offer she believed she couldn't refuse. Maybe she was wrong.

Jenny was one of those computer-geek/black-hats. She loved to get into places she didn't belong. She made a name for herself and was almost a legend. Those in the know knew her as 'Wonder Woman'. She was self-taught; a genius when it came to understanding computer codes and language. She learned everything about computers and programming in only two years. Ever since her sixteenth birthday when she got her first computer.

Within a month, she was known around the computer gaming circuit and was always atop leader boards. Soon she began experimenting with writing programs. In five, she invented an online game which was being played by so many people an on-line gaming company bought her program. She now possessed the money to build her own computer. One which was more powerful than anything sold in retail stores and better than most small companies.

In eight months, she was introduced by an online acquaintance to the world of hacking. It was a whole new challenge to get into places people didn't want you to go. She hacked into the Health Department and made a new birth certificate for herself. With that, she got into the mainframe of the Department of Motor Vehicles and got a driver's license with the fake birth date. She also got into a college computer and gave herself a degree in computer sciences.

Over the months, she became so hooked on hacking she was like a junkie on drugs. She couldn't get enough. She surprised herself with what she could do and went so far as to hack into a bank, creating false accounts for her and some friends.

One of those friends, a young teenager himself, got greedy and tried to withdraw too much from the bank, setting off inquiries about his age and the legitimacy of the account. He was caught and after being threatened with Federal Prison, he gave Jenny up as the source of the intrusion and all the information on the hacking. That kind of thing happens when you try to take out over ten thousand dollars at the drive through teller window while on a moped. He wasn't a genius.

A raid was conducted on her home and all her computers and files were confiscated. Her parents were unaware of what was happening. There were talks of charging them; having the house taken away; prison for many years. She just turned eighteen and for prosecution purposes, she was considered an adult.

While she was in custody, and before a trial date could be set, she was visited by a Mr. Cunningham. She believed him to be some government official. He made her an offer to come work with him. She would be able to put her computer skills to good use for the right purpose. If she did so for three months, all charges would be dropped, all records of her arrest would be expunged, no action would be taken against her family or the home, and she would have a computer workshop which Bill Gates would love.

She took the offer. She didn't have much choice then. Now, four months later, jail looked like it would have been the safest place for her.

When she was first taken to The Facility, she thought she was being taken straight to prison. She wasn't far from wrong. For security, the location was not disclosed. She was taken alone in the back of a van with no windows; at night.

The van was driven around in so many directions she had no idea which way she was headed. It seemed the drive took hours. When the van finally stopped and the back door opened, she found she was in what appeared to be a warehouse or a distribution center. She was taken inside through some hallways to a room with a table and some chairs. She was told someone would be with her soon. 'Soon' turned out to be about a half an hour if not more.

When the door opened, Mr. Cunningham came in. He was in an army uniform. A load of ribbons was on his chest and two stars on each of his shoulders. He put a folder on the table.

"Let me introduce myself one more time. I'm Major General Cunningham. I'm in charge of The Facility and the operations going on here. You are here because you are very good at what you do. But you can be replaced. There are certain rules which must be adhered to while you are here. Violating those rules will negate any agreement which we have and you will go directly back into police custody. He opened the folder and produced several papers. "These are non-disclosure agreements and release forms." He pulled a pen from inside his jacket. "Sign these," he said, not asking.

"What are they for?" she asked, beginning to read the forms.

"I just told you. Sign them or take the long ride back to jail."

She signed the forms grudgingly, not certain what all they said, but sure it had to do with keeping her mouth shut.

"What do you do here? What do you want me to do?"

"We do what we need to do; you do what we tell you. Welcome to the team. You will report directly to me. You will not have conversations with anyone else about your work, your life, past, present, or future, or anything having to do with The

Facility. You will have your duties and you will have your time off. There will be no leaving The Facility at any time. Everything you need will be provided. There will not be any outside contact except by my authorization. If you disobey these orders, you will be returned to police custody and face federal prosecution. I will have someone escort you to your quarters."

CHAPTER 21

Gillam and Lovett went down to the Communications Section. There were sections set up for each operator on the 911 system. There were separate sections for the dispatchers for each patrol zone and detectives, as well as the citywide camera network. They found Simmons there at a computer console.

"Hey, Simmons," Gillam greeted him. Lovett just gave a slight wave and nod of his head. Still not a big fan of his.

"Hi guys, any more strange stuff going on?" he asked.

"That wrecker driver who picked up the wrecked Medical Examiner's wagon is missing and the wrecker just turned up in the river. We need to get the report when it comes in. Have you been able to find out any more on the van or car?"

"Not a thing. I'm scared I dug too deep. Besides, I've hit a brick wall. There's nothing there. It's going to take more computer savvy than what I've got and I've got a good bit. The equipment here is primeval at best. You'd need state of the art stuff to get anywhere."

"We appreciate you helping out. Have you got time to check out our car with the GPS in it?" Gillam asked, seeing it was close to his getting off time. "Can you make absolutely sure there are no bugs in it?"

"Sure. I'd like to see that thing. Maybe I can get some

leads from it. It's fun playing the detective for a change. Any chance I can get a badge and gun?"

"You can forget that, Barney," Lovett said. "You'll use the badge to try to impress the girls and you'll just shoot yourself in the foot with the one bullet we'd reluctantly give you."

"Gillam, I'll deal with *you* on this," Simmons said in a huff. "Anything I come up with goes directly to you. Someone who appreciates my talents," he said, giving Lovett a sideways glance.

"That's fine," Gillam said with a smile. "He does stuff like that all the time. Means he likes you. Here's the key to the detective car," he said taking the key off his key ring and putting it beside the computer. It's parked in its usual place. I suggest you make sure it's not booby-trapped before you open anything. We'll take my personal car, after I make sure it's clear of any devices.

"Booby-trapped? Are you kidding me? I hope you're kidding me."

"I am too," Gillam said. "With everything going on, I'm almost expecting it. If you do find anything, you call me first. You don't talk to anyone and anyone asking what you're doing, you just tell them you're installing a radio in the car. It shouldn't be anybody's business anyway."

"Okay. Do you want me to remove the GPS or what?"

"Tell you what," Gillam continued. "call me when you've looked at it and I'll tell you what to do next."

"Right. But what if I get thrown in the back of a black van, or if I'm in small pieces by that time, then what happens to this one called Simmons?"

Lovett responded, "You'll get a plaque and maybe a bathroom or a closet named after you. I thought you were the 'man to go to', the 'count on me' guy?"

"I'm the 'I want to live' guy too. I don't mind helping you guys out. It's kind of fun, exciting, mysterious, and dangerous all rolled into one. It's better than sitting here running tags and wanted people while getting 911 calls because grandma misplaced her false teeth. I just don't want to wake up dead one morning."

"I don't think you need to worry too much," Gillam said. "If they're after anyone, it appears to be me and Sam. I don't know why and we still don't know who, but we're going to continue investigating."

"Tell it to Kim and the missing wrecker driver. What have they got to do with it? And who else we don't know about? I just don't want to be added to the list, that's all I'm saying."

"We don't either. Just keep things quiet and between us, and there shouldn't be any problem for you. We'll get to the bottom of all this and we'll keep you informed. Just don't forget to call when you find something out about the GPS."

After meeting with Simmons, Gillam and Lovett went out to the parking lot and checked Gillam's Hyundai Santa Fe for any booby-traps, bugs, or GPS devices. Nothing was found and both gave a sigh of relief. They then headed to the Medical Examiner's office.

Gillam called Dr. Higdon on his cell, and gave an ETA of about ten minutes. With the doctor's 'it's about time' attitude, he said he and Jaccob would be holding their breath. He then called Starling and told him they were on the way to the ME's office. He agreed to meet them there in about fifteen. Gillam reminded him to check his vehicle for any booby-traps or devices.

Starling would have laughed, but knew Gillam was being very serious. He would check and check well.

Gillam and Lovett arrived and found the front door locked. After Lovett pounded on it for a few minutes, Gillam saw a doorbell and pushed it. After a short wait, Jaccob came to the door and unlocked it.

"It be good to see you again, my friends," Jaccob said, flashing those big white teeth again and pushing out the monster sized hand.

"Hello Jaccob," they both said. Both gingerly took Jaccob's hand in turn, but he didn't crush them as they both anticipated. Gillam continued, "Is Doctor Higdon with you?"

"No. Doctor Higdon is in examining room."

"Yes, I mean he's here in the building with you?"

"Yes, that is what I have said. He is in examining room,

not here. We go and meet with him."

"Okay, in just a minute. We have another detective coming to meet with us here. Someone who is going to help us figure all this out. We'll just wait for him here so we can all be together at one time."

After a few minutes, Detective Starling drove up and parked. He got to the front door of the building just as it was opened for him by Jaccob. Starling looked up and his mouth dropped open as he walked in.

"Yeah, I know," Lovett said. "Same thing happened to me when I first saw him. Thanks for coming. Now we can get to work."

"Jaccob, this is Detective John Starling." Gillam made the introductions. "He's a homicide detective. He investigates when people die of un-natural causes. He's one of the good guys. John this is Jaccob Mutumbo, he's here to learn to be a medical examiner's assistant from Doctor Higdon. He'll take what he learns take back to his country."

Jaccob again held out his huge hand and said, "It be a pleasure to greet you, John Starling. Starling gave a glance over to Gillam and Lovett before putting his hand in that much danger. Finally, he stretched out his arm and Mutumbo took his hand and began shaking it. When Starling took his hand back, he looked to make sure it was still there and didn't get swallowed up by the hand nearly the size of a baseball glove.

"It's my pleasure to meet you," he said. He still couldn't take his eyes off the big guy. At least, he finally closed his mouth.

"Okay Jaccob," Gillam said. "Now we can meet with Doctor Higdon. Let's get this show on the road. Sorry Jaccob, that's just another one of those expressions." To Starling, he said, "You should be careful what you say to Jaccob. He takes things quite literal."

As they began to walk towards a corridor, Starling relayed to Gillam, "I checked out my car before driving over here. I didn't find anything. And on the way over, I even tried to make sure I wasn't followed by making some quick turns and going down some side streets. Is this thing really going in that direction?"

"We don't know. We have so many weird things going on and most seem tied together in some way. It's one of the reasons I wanted us to meet and go over what has happened so far. I think if we put our heads together we might be able to understand it better."

They got to examination room number one and Doctor Higdon was just finishing up with a corpse. He still wore bloody latex gloves. The naked body was on a metal table with a slight depression. Gillam noticed the large 'Y' shaped stitching on the chest before he even noticed the body was that of a male. Lovett turned so as not to have to look.

Jaccob introduced them, "This be my friends I talked to you about and new friend, John Starling."

"Of course, they are," said the doctor. "Excuse the mess. We're so shorthanded now I thought I would try to help catch up while we waited for you. Looks like you brought an army."

"This is my partner, Sam Lovett, and Detective John Starling from Homicide."

"Yes, Yes, I know Starling. Good man. You can't work homicide and not know the Medical Examiner. You, you and that partner of yours over there. I don't know you. You keep talking about safety. Okay, you're here. You said you had things to tell me. Spit it out man, don't choke on it."

"Well sir, I don't really know where to start. They say it's best to start at the beginning, but I don't really know where that is."

"Son, are you trying to get my goat?"

Mutumbo looked strangely at the doctor, "Goat?"

William N. Gilmore

CHAPTER 22

While Doctor Higdon cleaned up, Jaccob finished with the body and placed it in one of the refrigerated compartments. The group moved to a conference room where they all could sit down and everyone brought up to date on the events over the past few days.

Doctor Higdon came into the room followed by Jaccob.

"Okay son," the doctor said, "you're on. It's time to hear what the hell all this has to do with Doctor Kim and why things are being so secretive. And you better make it good."

Gillam got up and stood behind his chair. "First I want to say that I don't have all the answers. I'm not sure I have the right questions. Doctor Higdon here, says Kim was murdered. A gunshot to the head, so it appears the accident was staged and Kim's body burnt to cover it up. The wagon was found going away from the ME's office. Gasoline was used to accelerate the fire. The wagon ran on diesel." Gillam continued after a breath.

"The body Kim was transporting, the homeless guy who appeared to have overdosed, was missing. The body of the prostitute, Jessie, is missing from here along with records of her autopsy which Kim performed. Doctor Kim's office was ransacked and a gasoline booby-trap set. We've been followed by an unknown black car and a black van which appear to have government ties. A GPS unit was hidden in our detective car. The wrecker driver who picked up the wagon is missing, maybe dead, and the wrecker turned up in the river. Sam, is there anything I've missed?

"How weird Lieutenant Jones has been acting. And the missing drugs."

"Yeah, right. When the homeless guy was found, the patrolman who found him saw drugs next to him. The next person to be on the scene was Lieutenant Jones, the Narcotics Commander. After Jones left the scene, the drugs were missing. And it appeared he intentionally compromised the crime scene by covering up footprints in the house. He didn't want Homicide or us doing any investigation on the dead guy. And both the homeless guy and the prostitute appeared to have died the same way, but now we may never know. Now you have the Reader's Digest version of what is going on. Any questions or comments?"

Starling spoke up. "I have a contact in the FBI who's checking on the car and van, and who it may have been following you. I should have an answer soon."

Doctor Higdon spoke up next. "After you called, Jaccob was trying to tell me about everything which has happened including the booby-trap you mentioned. Sounds wicked. I don't know how they got in here. There's no forced entry and we don't have any security cameras. Which is something I'm definitely going to change. And the girl they took, Kim already completed the autopsy, but all his notes are gone, so I can't give any direct medical relation to the other body which is missing. Yes, in my opinion, Kim was murdered and the accident staged to cover it up. I didn't recover a bullet, but it appears to have been a .38 or a 9mm, or something real close. Not a hollow point. The angle of the entry wound on the left side of the head and exit wound near the right temple suggests the person who fired the shot was slightly behind and lower than Kim, and about three to five feet away."

"Kim was only about five foot six. Are you saying were looking for a midget who likes to sneak up from behind and shoot people?" Lovett asked.

Doctor Higdon gave him a stern look. "Don't get on my bad side now, boy. I said what I said and now it's time for someone else to figure out what happened. I want to know who killed Kim, and I want to know who was willing to burn down our building to cover up their theft of the body and the autopsy report."

"Look doc," Lovett said. "I want to know these things too. I want to know how they all fit together. And I want to know why some people are so interested in our activities; who can we trust and who's out to get us?"

"First, don't ever call me, 'Doc'. I'm Doctor, Doctor Higdon, Mr. Higdon, and to a very few, I'm Charles. You may use either of the first two. Second, what is your department doing about this mess?"

"We haven't informed anyone else of the findings yet," Gillam answered. "We believe there may be others, including high ranking officers, who either know what's going on, are involved in what's going on, or are looking the other way. Like I said, we don't know whom to trust right now, except everyone in this room. Detective Starling trusts his FBI contact and that's good enough for me. We may need someone like that on the outside who can do some things we can't and has better resources. Which is why we're meeting here. Everyone must be on their toes. That means be alert, Jaccob," he added.

"Try not to be alone. Be careful of what you say on the phone and to others. Keep checking your cars, office, home, and check to see if you're being followed or watched. It may sound like I'm asking you to be paranoid, and I guess to some degree I am, but it may be what keeps you alive."

"Okay, now you've qualified your 'safety' remarks," the doctor replied. "But where does the investigation go from here?"

"I think we should take it very slowly," Gillam answered. "We document everything. We piece it together like a puzzle. We secure any evidence we find and keep a chain of evidence just in case there is something here which goes to court. Just like any other case, we need to have solid evidence. We can't just go off half-cocked with speculation and conjecture or we'll look like fools, or like we're out to get someone, maybe both. And if there is anything to all this, we need to be able to make a solid arrest and get a conviction in court."

"You said you believe the black car and van which were following you has *government ties*, the doctor inquired. "If so, what is the government involvement? Which agency of the government?"

"Believe me, I've asked the same questions and so far, I don't have any answers. I'm waiting on the FBI contact to fill in the blanks if he can. I have someone checking on some other information for me, but I'm not comfortable enough to bring him into the fold. He's a little bit of a loose cannon and his mouth is bigger than his brain sometimes; however, he really wants to help."

"All right," the doctor said, "I'll go along with your plan. For now, that is. There must be some progress made. Soon. I can't just sit on this information about Doctor Kim and the rest of what has happened here. I'll lose my license for sure and that's not going to happen. What do we do in the mean time?"

"I suggest you keep Jaccob close by as your personal body guard. He has a nose, no pun intended, for sniffing out danger and I suspect he has some training in that respect. He saved our butts from the booby-trap and he's very intimidating."

Jaccob just sat there with a big grin, nodding his head. Gillam believed he was a lot more than just an orderly in training. He also suspected Jaccob understood a lot more than he let on.

"The rest of us will do our thing. Following up all the leads we can. Sam and I have a couple of off days ahead. I don't know who's watching us or what their plan is. If they wanted us dead, they missed their chance. I'd rather not give them another. I suspect they will keep doing what they're doing, but if we change our ways, it may cause them to react in ways we don't want. I suggest we try to live our lives as close to what they would have been if none of this was happening."

"I'm releasing Doctor Kim's body to his wife, unless you think there is any reason to hold it," Doctor Higdon said. "I think there may be a service for him in a couple of days. That's something I intend to be a part of and nobody is going to intimidate me to keep me away."

"I don't think we need to keep her waiting any longer," Gillam agreed. "Just make sure you have all the documentation on the autopsy copied and safe."

"I've already done so, son. I'm no idiot."

"No sir, you're not, and I know I don't need to tell you how to do your job. It's just that I want to make sure in my own mind I have everything covered. I don't want anyone else hurt and I don't want these guys getting away with anything. There's been too much of that, especially in the government. I don't have too much longer till retirement and I'd rather get there on my feet."

Gillam's phone rang.

"Hey Gillam, Simmons here. I didn't find any bugs in your car and the GPS unit doesn't have any markings. If there had been a serial number on the outside of it, it's been removed.

The only thing I can do is take it out and see what's inside it."

"Leave it there for now. The car won't be moved for a couple days while were off. Hold on to the key and I'll get it from you later."

"You might also want to get some air freshener. When I opened the trunk, it smelled like someone died in there."

"Okay, I'll ..., Simmons, you're a genius. Don't let anyone ever tell you different." Gillam hung up. "That's funny, he's the genius and we're the idiots, Sam."

"Speak for yourself. Simmons a genius? That'll be the day."

"Sam, we've already got some evidence. The board from the abandoned house. The one with the bloody handprints on it. The blood sample I took from it and turned in. We've got something for the doctor to examine. Blood from the homeless guy."

"My God, you're right. I forgot too. But then again, we don't have anything to compare it with. Jessie's body is gone along with the report. No way to say they died the same way or to say they are even involved with all this mess."

"No, but it's a start. And don't forget the sample of burnt tire with the gas residue. I wouldn't be surprised if the gas in the light bulb isn't the same."

"Doc, oops, sorry," Lovett announced, a little red faced. "Doctor Higdon, if we got you a sample of the blood from the homeless man, is there any way to tell how he died?"

"Most likely not. It depends on a number of factors. I can do a toxicology test on the blood as well as a few others depending on the size of the sample; however, it won't tell me if he died of a shooting, a stabbing or any other types of assault or accidents."

"Kim told us the girl died of what appeared to be a total body hemorrhage. Like nothing he had ever seen before. It may have been an overdose from some drugs she smoked or ingested. Have you ever heard of anything like that?"

"The closest thing I can think of right now is decompression sickness. You call it the bends. Most notable in divers using scuba tanks with mixed gases of oxygen and nitrogen. The nitrogen gets released into the blood and organs as bubbles caused by returning to the surface too quickly and not allowing them to dissolve over time; which is why you see divers stop several times on the way to the surface after a deep dive. Unlike oxygen, the body doesn't use the nitrogen; it gets stored in the tissues and then released too quickly. Think about shaking up a bottle of soda and then opening the top right away. You have a real mess, but if you wait long enough you can open it safely."

"So, what you're saying," Lovett questioned, "is the two got their tops popped open too quickly after smoking some dope laced with nitrogen?"

"No, nothing quite like that. Ingesting small amounts of nitrogen wouldn't cause it. We breathe in nitrogen every day.

Some more than others if they smoke or work in certain environments. I'm saying *something* caused their systems to, if you wish, pop. I'm not saying it was some narcotic or what it was until I can do some testing myself."

William N. Gilmore

CHAPTER 23

When the meeting was about over, Starling got Gillam alone and told him he appreciated the confidence in his contact choice. He didn't go into a lot of detail about how they met, but he did tell him he was someone whom they could count on. He gave him Tommy's name and number just in case he needed to contact him directly.

"So, what are your plans for this weekend?" Starling asked.

"It looks like I'm going to a ballgame," Gillam said. "Surround myself with lots of people."

"If I get any word from Tommy, do you want me to call you or wait until you are back to work? Starling asked.

"No, call me anytime," Gillam said. "I'd rather have the information as fresh as possible. In fact, I'm anxious for it."

"I'll do that then," Starling agreed. "I'm going to head over to the kid's house who called me and told me he was in the house with the dead guy. See what information he can add. He sounded like a good kid. Maybe I can work a little magic on him and get him going in the right direction and not down the gang road. Want to go and see what he says?"

"I think Sam and I will do some more follow up before we get off. There's something I want to get back to. I have a hunch and usually I need to follow those. Good luck with him."

"Thanks. Catch you later." Starling said his goodbyes to everyone and left.

"Doctor Higdon," Gillam said, as he and Lovett walked up to him. "I want to thank you for listening to me and understanding where I was going with this thing. My main concern right now is everyone's safety and then finding out who is behind everything."

"Son, you did good explaining what you believed. Sorry I gave you a hard time earlier. I just don't know how you're going to put it all together and make a case against a shadow hiding in the night."

"Right now, I don't either. I won't give up though. Neither will Lovett. He's a good man. He's very sarcastic and cynical at times and often gets carried away. I left his leash and muzzle in the car."

"He doesn't bother me. Not too much anyway."

"There is something I wanted to ask you though, if you don't mind. It's about Jaccob."

"Okay, shoot."

"He made mention once that he was a soldier. He appears to have some knowledge of certain tactics. Can you shed any light on this? Do you know much about his background?"

"I know he comes from a small African country which is involved in a civil war. His country is being torn apart by warlords who want to get rich on drugs, diamonds and human trafficking. I also know he is the son of one of the opposition leaders. He fought against some of those warlords and their forces. I think one of them is an uncle," the doctor added.

"He was badly wounded in the fighting and taken care of by missionaries. He learned his English while recuperating and turned to Christianity and denounced the fighting. He continued his education and from the experiences with the missionaries, he became a medical student. As part of his education he was given a grant, I am sure his father was behind it, to come to America and further his education in the medical field. Something which was in jeopardy if he stayed in his country."

"He obviously has skills," Gillam said.

"How much military training he has, I have no idea," Doctor Higdon continued. "I do know he does whatever is asked of him. He works hard and although he is paid very little, he sends almost all his money home. He has few if any real friends which I know of and he lives in a small apartment not far from here, but most nights you can find him right here. He is either working, reading, or watching. He has only been here a couple of weeks and already he is further ahead of any student who ever worked for me in the past."

"Well, that answers that," Gillam said. "How long do you have him?"

"Just a couple more months. He returns home and I hope continues his schooling until he gets his internship. I would love to have him back."

"He's a very nice guy. He's a very big guy. I just can't see him as a doctor. He looks more like a basketball player. I wonder if he plays."

"Oh yes, very well too. I think that is one of the ways he recuperated and built his strength back up. There's a goal in the back parking lot which he sometimes uses."

"When all this is over, I wonder if I could be his agent."

"Sorry. I've already got dibs."

"Well then, I guess I'll have to keep being a cop for a while. Come on Sam. We have some more crap to do today before we get off. That didn't come out right, did it?"

Sam laughed and said, "Yeah, I think it came out exactly right." He and Gillam headed for the door. Jaccob was right there and before you could say *"boo"*, Jaccob grabbed both men, lifting them up in a big bear hug.

"I thank you for what you do. Go and God be with you." He let the men go and they both could have sworn they dropped a foot. They both smiled at Jaccob and both in turn said "And with you, Amen."

When the detectives reached Gillam's car, Lovett asked him where he wanted to go next.

"We're headed back to the impound lot," Gillam said. "I have a hunch about something and want to check it out."

"You want to fill me in or are you going to keep treating me like a mushroom?"

"Two things actually," Gillam began, "First, did you

happen to notice if the keys to the wagon were still in the ignition?"

"No. I didn't even think to look for them."

"I think that's how they got into the Medical Examiner's office and then into Kim's office without force. They used Kim's keys. I want to be sure though."

"And second?" Sam asked.

"Second, I want to see if there is a bullet or a bullet hole somewhere in the driver's compartment of the wagon. If Kim was sitting in the wagon when he was shot, according to Doctor Higdon, the person who shot him needed to be lower than he was. The wagon sits a good bit higher than a car. When Kim left with the homeless guy, his driver's side window was down. The AC was broken. I believe they may have been sitting in the passenger seat or right rear seat in a vehicle which pulled up beside him while he was stopped. He never saw it coming. He wasn't looking at or talking to anyone, he was looking straight ahead. Any blood in the compartment would have been attributed to the accident if it wasn't burnt away."

"You're scary when you get on a roll like this," Sam said. "Scary good that is. Now can you tell me who it is so we can go home?"

"I'm not that good," Gillam corrected, "I just put some things together in my head and tried to figure it out."

"Well there's enough room in there to unfold a world map, so I guess there's room for a puzzle or two. I'm glad you're my partner."

"Just remember that the next time I cause you to spill your coffee in your lap."

"There's going to be a next time? Sam asked. "I wonder if there's any kind of insurance I can get to protect me from you. You're dangerous."

The drive over to the impound yard didn't take long. Granger was still there at his office. He was waiting for the flat bed wrecker recovered in the river to be brought back to the yard. It needed to be removed by a crane and was being towed back. The wrecker was empty. No body was found in the river at the site it went in or downstream. The driver, Thompson, was still missing with no idea where to find him.

Granger was sitting there talking to a half bottle of whiskey. They believed they knew where the other half went.

"Mr. Granger, we need to look at the Medical Examiner's wagon one more time if you don't mind."

"No, I don't mind. I don't mind having a driver missing. I don't mind having a ruined wrecker. I don't even mind getting the run-a-round about what's going on. What I do mind is the fact no one seems to care. No one is even concerned one iota about a man's life. He may be hurt, he may be dying, he may be in a bar getting liquored up, but no one seems to care about one little ole wrecker driver. Not the police, not the public, not even the newspapers." He took a big swig from the bottle. "Oh yeah, I called the newspapers. I told them how he went missing after all this crap started with the arson of the Medical Examiner's wagon. Did they seem to care? I guess not. No one has called me back. No one bothered to come here. So, do I mind if you want to look at a beat-up wreck? Hell, no, knock yourself out."

There was no need to talk with him anymore. They were sure the conversation would have been even less coherent in a short time. They went out to where the wagon was located. A big blue tarp was placed over the cab section of the wagon because the windows were all busted out. Lovett, because of his size, was selected by default to climb into the now compressed cab. Part of the steering wheel was melted as was some of the dash. The front seats were just scorched frames. He first checked the ignition switch.

"No keys," he yelled out to Gillam. He was probably right about Kim's keys being used to gain entry to the Medical Examiner's office, he thought. Now, the almost impossible task of finding a bullet in all this mess. No way to use a metal detector and he wished he could have made a sifter box. He was forced to do it the old fashion way. With his eyes and fingers.

The ash and soot were still damp and made a nasty type of paste. He needed to be careful of broken glass and sharp metal fragments. He hoped there could be an easier way, but there wasn't. He thought about Kim sitting in the driver's seat and the angle of the bullet as described by the Do …, he caught himself, by Doctor Higdon.

He imagined a line. A line which went from the entry wound to the exit wound of Kim's head as he sat in the driver's seat. The line of travel of the bullet after leaving Kim's head would have it going into the headliner just above the windshield between the driver's seat and the passenger seat. Almost everything was burnt away. There was no longer a headliner.

Lovett felt around the area and found a small dent in the metal of the inside roof of the cab. He smiled. Doctor Higdon knew just what he was talking about. The indenture had a slight upside down tear drop outline. This indicated to him the bullet traveled downwards after hitting the metal. He began checking from that position down and although part of the dash had melted and was charred black, he looked real close and found a small hole in the un-cracked plastic.

"Hey Gillam," he yelled. "Gillam," a little louder that time.

"What? Did you find something?"

"I'm not sure yet. You got a knife on you?"

"No, you know they won't let me carry anything sharp. Just kidding, I have one in the car. I'll get it."

Gillam returned with a large lock-blade knife and handed it to Lovett, handle first and blade opened. "What have you got?"

"I'm not sure yet. Give me a minute."

Gillam heard Lovett working away at something inside the cab, causing the whole wreck to shake.

"What are you doing in there, wrestling a bear?"

After several minutes, Lovett popped his head out. "No bears in here. Just miners. I had to do some digging. Here's your knife," handing it to Gillam handle first, the same way he got it, blade opened. "And here's a nice 9mm slug," also handing that over to Gillam. The 9mm slug was in relatively good shape except slightly dented on the front tip and on one side. Lovett did a good job getting it out of the plastic dash without gouging it or causing any other damage to the slug.

Gillam was pleased. "Great work. It might be good enough for ballistics testing. Where was it?"

Lovett was climbing out of the wagon. "It had hit the roof and ricocheted down into the dash. It was buried in the cushioning of the dash. Lucky the fire didn't destroy more of the dash or we may never have found it."

"Don't say *we*," Gillam said. "You found it. Now we have something to add to our little collection of things."

"It was your idea," Lovett said. "Maybe you should be putting in those transfers and go work in Homicide."

"No thanks," Gillam said, shaking his head. "brush yourself off, we need to pick up that board with the bloody handprints at the property section and take it over to Doctor Higdon along with this bullet."

"You think he can tell something from the blood?" Sam asked.

"I think the man might be able to clone Kim and bring him back if he had a mind to. And I wouldn't be the person to tell him he couldn't."

"Yeah, I know what you mean," Sam said. "He reminds me of someone."

"Me too," Gillam agreed. "My father and grandfather."

"No, nothing like that," Sam said. "He reminds me of Sean Connery. Not the *007, James Bond*, Connery, but the one from the *Untouchables*.

"Like I said," Gillam nodded. "my father and grandfather."

"What happened to you?" Sam asked, with a laugh, "You're more like *Agent 86, Maxwell Smart*. And now you work for the *Keystone Cops*.

"Okay, enough of this old movie crap," Gillam insisted. "Let's go finish this day out. By the way, if you can get the tickets for Sunday, you can call Debbie and tell her I'm up for the ballgame this weekend. I need the distraction."

"Now you're talking, Lovett said with a smile. "I'm sure you'll have a good time. Are you sure though your cat won't mind?"

Larry gave Sam a look which stopped his smiling, and said dead serious, "You want to get thrown back in that wagon or have a new one pick you up?"

The detectives covered the wagon again with the tarp and before leaving stopped to check in with Granger. Granger was asleep or passed out, head down with the now empty whisky bottle lying on the desk.

CHAPTER 24

They arrived at the Atlanta Police Property section and Gillam was signing out the board he previously placed in as evidence just the evening before.

The property clerk, dressed in a blue jump suit, was a young officer neither Gillam nor Lovett recalled seeing before. He was helping them while another was standing in the back near the storage area.

"Excuse me, detective, I need your identification to make a copy for the property transfer."

"No problem," Gillam said, getting his billfold out. "Are you new here at property? I don't remember seeing you here before."

"Yes sir, this is my first full day here. I just got out of the academy and I guess they were shorthanded. I got assigned here along with the other officer from my class. I was really hoping to get on the street first thing."

"Well I'm sure it won't be long; we need officers on the street pretty bad too." Gillam handed the officer his identification along with the property release form.

He went over to the copy machine and returned shortly with Gillam's identification. "It will be just a few minutes. I'll be right back." He headed to the back of the evidence storage area and the other officer followed him.

Gillam and Lovett hung out in the property receiving area waiting on the officer.

They waited and continued to wait. After about fifteen minutes, they wondered if there was a problem. Luckily, no one else entered with anything to turn in.

"I wonder what's taking so long." Lovett inquired. "It shouldn't take this long for two people to find and get one board."

Gillam went over to a buzzer used to summon the clerks when they were in the back and someone entered for service. He pressed the buzzer and heard it ringing in the back. There was no answer. He pressed it again, a little longer this time. After a few minutes, there was still no answer. One more time on the buzzer; this time he pressed it for an extended period, released it, and pressed it several times in succession. He followed this up by yelling for the clerks. There was no answer from any attempt.

Gillam and Lovett looked at each other. They drew their weapons and began a careful entry into the storage area. Gillam again yelled for the clerks. Nothing, but echoes. Gillam pointed at Lovett and directed him to one side of the entrance and gave him some more hand signs that, as partners, they learned to use so as not to give away their positions, tactics, or numbers.

They moved up in a leapfrog movement. Gillam moved up, cleared an area, and motioned Lovett to move up. Lovett moved up further and then motioned Gillam to move up. They did this until the area was completely cleared. No sign of the clerks. No sign of anyone. All the access doors were locked. All the office doors were locked.

Gillam speculated, "Either the clerks went into an office and locked the doors behind them, or they exited the building and the doors self-locked behind them. Either way it's mighty strange. Why would they just leave like that while they were trying to help us?"

"They could have been beamed up," Lovett said.

"I might even consider that if we don't find an answer here real soon. Let's give it the once over one more time. If we don't find something, then we'll need to call someone. We can't just leave the evidence and property unsecured."

"I agree with you there. Let's start at the front again and work our way to the back. Check every door, nook and—" A faint sound drew Lovett's attention. A 'Did you hear that?' look passed between them. Gillam, pointed towards the noise. Lovett nodded.

They worked their way towards the location and could hear some more noise. Not sure what was making the noise or why, they proceeded very carefully.

They came to an area where some large cardboard boxes were stacked. They heard the noise there. It was a muffled, scratching sound. They moved up to the boxes and Lovett, moving one of the boxes expected to see a large rat. Instead, behind the box he saw a blue jump-suited figure with duct tape wrapped around his mouth, eyes, and whole head. His hands and feet were taped together in a hog-tied fashion. He was alone.

They moved in and began unwrapping him. The tape was strong and they tried to be careful taking it off his face, especially his eyes. The whole time they were doing this they were talking to him trying to assure him he was safe now and they were there to help. They got it off his mouth and he began coughing, trying to catch his breath. He almost threw-up right there. Gillam recognized him as one of the regular property clerks who had been assigned there for years.

"Peterson, it's Detective Gillam. What the hell is going on here?"

"What happened?" Larry asked, as they untied his hands and feet.

Peterson, still coughing, was trying to talk in between gasps for air. He was rubbing his wrist as he sat up.

"There were two of them. Owww," he yelled, as the tape was being removed, pulling out hair.

"Sorry," Gillam said, "I'll let you get it yourself. Are you hurt anywhere?"

"Only my pride for letting them take me down. I've gotten soft working here. I thought they were a couple of recruits sent over to help with inventory. I turned my back to them and the next thing I know, I'm on the floor and being tied up with duct tape. They couldn't use rope. No, they had to go and use something sticky, the bastards."

"Did they say what they wanted?" Gillam asked, helping Peterson to his feet.

"Once they took me down, they didn't talk with me at all. I heard them mumbling to each other, but I couldn't make it out. I think they went out the back door. I don't know what they took, if anything, and I don't know any reason why they would do something like this. As you know, we don't store any drugs or money back here. It's kept separate in secure areas. Guns are kept in locked cabinets." Feeling his pocket, he said, "I still have my keys. Did you see any forced entries into anything?"

"No, but I think we did see your two attackers. We saw at least one fairly well. Young guy, maybe twenty-three to twenty-five or six. About six foot, blondish brown hair. More of a southern accent."

"You talked to him?" Wincing as he pulled more tape from his hair.

"Yeah, I thought he was a new clerk. Fresh out of the academy. That's what he said anyway. Seemed to know what he was doing. Fooled me too. I didn't get a good look at the other guy. He hung in the back shadows."

"Fooled me as well," Lovett added. "It's possible the other guy was armed. You may have gotten lucky."

"We need to call the property commander and tell him," Peterson said, heading for the phone. "I need to make a police report on this. You two need to stay and be witnesses."

Gillam thought for a second, "Can you hold that up for a

just a bit?"

"What? Are you out of your ever-loving mind? Wait for what?"

"I want to check on something. I think I know what they took," Gillam stated."

"How could you know that? What's going on here anyway?"

"Can you check on a piece of property for me first? If it's what I think then we might need to make some other arrangements."

"Other arrangements?" Peterson repeated. "Why do all you guys talk in riddles and codes when something is going on and you don't have a clue what it is? Just tell me what you want and I'll tell you what I want in return."

Gillam and Lovett looked at each other. How could they argue with that?

"Okay, you win," Gillam agreed. "I need to check on a plywood board and some tire pieces I brought in yesterday. The board had some bloody handprints on it. It may be evidence from a, ah …, a crime."

"All right, I'll play along for now," Peterson said. "Follow me."

They went back to the front where property and evidence are received. Peterson went to a computer and almost began to type up the search for the items.

"I'll be a …, here it is right here. They already brought it up on the computer. Come on. Let's go look." They followed Peterson again going back to the storage area. He went down one isle and crossed over, going down another until he stopped and began looking around.

"Yep, that's it! That's what they took. They're gone. Why?" he asked, staring at the detectives with a bewildered look.

"Because it was another piece of the puzzle," Gillam answered.

"You are lucky," Lovett said.

"How's that?" Peterson asked.

"There's another piece of evidence which ended up missing; evidence in the form of a body. Somebody killed to get that piece of evidence. It's all very complicated and we can't tell you all of it right now, so let's get down to it. We want these guys bad. Real bad. We're working on it. We don't want too much getting out about what we're doing, what we've found, or any of it. Not the press, not our supervisors, we're not even telling our wives and girlfriends." Gillam looked questioningly at Lovett on that one. "Now, you're part of it. We need your co-operation. We need this kept quiet. What's it going to cost us?"

William N. Gilmore

CHAPTER 25

Detective Starling pulled up to the address of Curtis Harris. He called right after leaving the Medical Examiner's office and got permission from Curtis' aunt to come right over. She was quite concerned about Curtis and his activities. She was relieved he wasn't in any trouble and welcomed the fact that someone was taking an interest.

He got to the door and was about to knock when the door opened and a young boy looked up at him and said "Hi."

"Hi, yourself. I'm Detective John Starling. You must be Curtis?"

The young boy looked outside first one way then the other to see who was watching.

John took a step back to give the boy some room so he could see who was being nosey.

The coast must have been clear. "Yes sir, that be me. Come on inside." After John crossed the threshold, the boy looked out one more time before closing the door.

"It's good to meet you Curtis. Is your aunt here?"

"Yeah, she'll be down in a minute. You got a gun?"

Starling was taken aback for a second. "Yes, of course, I'm a policeman." He pulled out his badge to show Curtis. He'd been asked about his gun before by youngsters, but never in such a direct way. Usually it was asked if he had ever shot anyone or been shot. He'd always had a problem with those, but he always gave a quick answer; No.

"I ain't in no trouble, am I?" Curtis asked.

"Not if you told me the truth. All the truth."

"I did. Well, after I fibbed the first time, that is. I was scared."

A woman was making her way down the steps. A lovely woman.

"Hello," she said.

"Hello, I'm Detective John Starling. I'm here to talk with Curtis' aunt. Will she be available soon?"

"I'm Curtis' aunt. I'm Ms. Dorothy Harris."

She was stunning. About the same age as Starling, late thirties, early forties. Tall, well proportioned, wearing a very nice blue dress.

"Oh, excuse me, I was told you …, ah …, or rather, Curtis' aunt was old, I mean you, I mean she, was an older lady." John stumbled at his attempt to make an explanation.

"Well, these young people think anyone over thirty-five is beyond prime nowadays and when you get close to fifty, it's time to go into a home. I'm not quite ready for that yet."

"I should say not," John said, blushing a little as he realized his statement could be interpreted as flirting; maybe it was.

"You'll have to excuse Curtis' manners. Please, have a

seat. He told me what happened at the abandoned house and that he called and talked with you. Is there more?"

"Thank you," he said, sitting on a sofa with Curtis, across from her. "First, Curtis is not in any trouble. In fact, he helped us out. I know it was a harrowing experience and I want to make sure he's handling it without any problems. I know something like that could bring up bad memories or cause nightmares, even feelings of guilt."

Looking over at Curtis, his aunt asked, "Curtis, are there any problems you want to tell us about? We've encountered these types of conversations before. You know it's all right to talk about things which bother you."

"There ain't no problems. It don't bother me none to see no dead guys."

"Curtis! What did I tell you about your language? You do not live in a ghetto. At school and here at home, you are taught the proper way to speak. Then you get out there in the street and around those friends of yours and you get to talking like that. You know better. You've been brought up better." Turning to Starling, she said, "I'm sorry, detective. I've tried to make sure he's taught properly and he doesn't get involved with those gangs and thugs out here, but sometimes it breaks my heart to think I'm wasting my time."

"I'm sorry, Aunt Dorothy," Curtis said, looking down. "I didn't think before I opened my mouth. Let me try again, please?" He looked up and straight at Starling. "No sir, there are no problems. I saw the dead man and it did not bother me."

Starling was impressed with the way his aunt handled the young boy. It was obvious she cared and was concerned with his upbringing.

"Thank you, Curtis. That was my main concern. One other thing you told me on the phone was that you saw some drugs and a crack pipe next to the man. Do you remember that?"

"Yes sir. There were some bags with crack cocaine and a pipe next to him. I didn't touch him or the drugs."

"Curtis, you didn't tell me about any drugs," his aunt said.

"I remembered when I was talking with the detective. I promise I didn't touch them. I don't mess with drugs. I know they're bad."

"I believe you, sweetheart."

"I believe you too, Curtis," John said. "Is there anything else you can remember from that day at the abandoned house?"

"I don't think so. I didn't know he was in there. I just wanted some wood for the fort we were—" then realizing he again opened his mouth before thinking. This time letting out the biggest secret of all.

"What fort?" Aunt Dorothy asked, raising her eyebrows.

"Ah, a fort me and the guys built."

"And where is this fort?" She continued to inquire.

"Looking down again, he mumbled, "In the woods."

"In the woods? What do you think …,"

"Ms. Harris, excuse me for butting in, but all young boys want a fort, or a tree house, or some 'Fortress of Solitude' to be able to call their own. Someplace to hang out, hide, pretend, and play. Maybe some areas are better than others, but it's not a gang hideout. It's not a pool hall, or a liquor store. Maybe, what it needs though is an *official* inspection to declare it safe and habitable," he continued giving a wink he hoped Curtis didn't see. "Maybe it's something I can do."

Curtis was looking at Starling with full admiration. The man is *King Solomon* and *Santa Claus* rolled into one, he thought.

Aunt Dorothy saw the look too. It had been a long time since there was a positive male role model for Curtis.

"I'm not real pleased you did this without telling me. I'll have to think about this for a while. But maybe, just maybe, if Detective Starling has some time and he says it's safe, then I may consider allowing you to have this fort. But it's not a hideout. You have to do your chores, keep your room clean, and watch the way you talk. If you can do those things, it will go a long way for me to think you're responsible enough to have a fort. Is that clear?"

"Oh, yes ma'am. Thank you." Turning towards Starling again. "Thank you, Detective."

"Please, both of you, call me John."

William N. Gilmore

CHAPTER 26

After making a deal with Peterson, Gillam and Lovett headed for the crime lab to get the blood sample Gillam swabbed from the plywood board. The sample would have been held at the crime lab until they were notified by the investigating officer that a certain suspect, or a victim of a crime, or other evidence was identified and a comparison check needed to be made. Or the sample was no longer needed and destroyed. At least they still retained the sample for Doctor Higdon to check.

"Who would be so brazen as to assault an officer right here in our own territory?" Lovett asked. "And then steal a piece of evidence right from under our noses? It makes no sense."

"Don't forget they killed Kim to get the body in the wagon and set a booby-trap at the Medical Examiner's office. That makes even less sense," Gillam returned. "I keep going over and over everything I know so far and there are so many holes I just can't get a grasp on it yet. I know it's right there. I can almost reach it. Just a few more pieces of the puzzle and I'll be able to see what the picture is."

"Just make sure we're not the ones full of holes if you don't mind," Sam stated. "I don't fancy becoming Swiss cheese."

The drive to the crime lab included several out of the way side streets, quick turns, and looks for black cars and vans.

Several black vehicles made the two detectives give second looks, but they were not the same vehicles from before. They even made sure there were no black helicopters keeping an eye from the sky. Caution was more prevalent than paranoia; however, it wasn't far behind.

At the crime lab, Gillam and Lovett went into the lobby, showed their police identification and signed in. They were given temporary visitor's badges. One of the techs was called down to assist them.

When the tech arrived and Gillam advised why they were there, they were escorted to one of the labs. The tech went to a logbook and checked for the evidence under a sign in procedure. The tech returned to the detectives and told Gillam the sample had already been signed out.

"Signed out? By whom?"

"By you. Not too long ago. Here it is," showing Gillam the logbook. "As a matter-of-fact, it was only about half an hour ago. It was released by Mr. Hernandez, one of the scientists."

"Well here I am." Gillam pulled his police identification out again and showed it to the tech. "This is me. I was not here before. I want to speak with this Mr. Hernandez. Right now!"

The tech retreated and returned shortly with a short Hispanic man in a white lab coat.

"I am Mr. Hernandez. What seems to be the problem?"

"Do you know me? Have you ever seen me before?" Gillam asked.

"No, I don't believe I have. What's going on?"

"The tech here says about a half hour ago, you released a blood sample which I turned in as evidence yesterday. He said you released it to me."

"I released a blood sample back to a Detective Gillam. I verified his identity and I have a copy of his identification. We are required to make copies of ID's and I have it in the file. Just a minute and I'll get it."

Mr. Hernandez returned with a file and produced a full sheet of paper with a copy of an Atlanta Police identification card on it. The card appeared to be official with the name of Larry Gillam on it, but the picture on the card was not his. There was something familiar about the picture though. Immediately it dawned on him. It was the so-called clerk from the property section. He remembered now that the guy made a copy of his identification before disappearing.

"So, this is the guy who signed out the sample?" showing the copy of the ID card to Mr. Hernandez.

"Yes, that's him. Seemed like such a nice young man too."

"Was he alone?"

"Yes."

"Please tell me you tested the sample, or maybe separated it and have a small bit left."

"No, I'm sorry. There was no need at the time to test it. Besides, we're so far behind it may have taken several weeks before we did once we received the information to do so."

"We're screwed," Lovett said, dejected.

"Yeah, and we didn't even get kissed," Gillam acknowledged.

CHAPTER 27

Lieutenant Jones answered the call on his cell phone after checking the digital display to make sure it was someone he wanted to talk with.

"This is Jones," he said.

"We've got both items. No real problems. We were able to use the ID just as you said. There are some real idiots working with you guys."

"Don't underestimate everyone you come across. Somehow they found the booby-trap in the Medical Examiner's office and that didn't exactly make me happy. What do you mean no *real* problems?"

"I don't like having my face seen and shown around. I can understand having to put my picture on the ID, but I didn't like leaving them a copy of it. Most people who see me learn to forget one way or another."

"It couldn't be helped. No one is going to be able to identify you. I was told you don't exist. There are no records or history for you. That's why you were chosen. Did you take care of both bodies as I told you?"

"Yes. Just as you said. No trace."

"Good. That's one loose end taken care of. We may have several more to deal with before this thing may be over."

Gillam got on the phone and gave the bad news to Doctor
Higdon. He wasn't very happy with the situation. He then called
Detective Starling and did the same. Starling was still at the
Harris home talking with Curtis and his Aunt Dorothy about the
Junior Police Program. He said he was just a couple blocks from
the house on Griffin Street if they wanted him to go over and
check the area again. They thought that might be a good idea
even though they had gone over the house pretty well. It might
be the only idea left. They agreed to meet him there in about
twenty minutes.

"Curtis, with your aunt's permission, would you show me
just what you did at the abandoned house? I'm meeting a couple
other detectives over there and we just want to make sure we
have all the facts and don't forget anything."

"Curtis, do you feel up to going with Detective Starling,
John, to the house one more time?" Aunt Dorothy asked. "You
don't have to if you don't feel right about it."

"I'll go. Can we stop at the fort?" he said beaming. "I
want to show it to you."

"Sure. I think we can make time. Ms. Harris, did you
want to go with us?"

"It's going to be dinner time shortly. I have to do some
cooking, so I'll just stay here. Would you care to join us?"

John didn't want to push it. "I'd love to, however, I still
have a lot of work to do. Would you mind if I take you up on that

at a later date?"

"Not at all. And please, call me Dorothy."

Curtis was disappointed John couldn't stay for dinner, but he still gave a slight smile when he heard the word *date*.

John and Curtis drove over to Griffin Street first so as not to miss the other detectives. When they pulled up and stopped on the street by the house, Curtis looked at the house remembering the events in a flashback, not hearing John speaking to him.

"Curtis? Curtis! Are you all right with this? We don't have to go in there. We don't even have to stay if you don't want."

"I'm okay. It just gives me the willies."

"You know they took him out of there. There's nothing in there. See, there's still the yellow crime scene tape around the house."

"Yes sir, I see. Things just bring back some memories sometimes."

"Yes, I know about bad memories. They're hard to deal with. It's good if you have someone to talk to about them."

"You have bad memories too?"

"Yes. Terrible ones. Sometimes I have nightmares. Sometimes I—"

Gillam and Lovett pulled up then and the conversation stopped short. Both John and Curtis exited the car.

"What's this, the department's new detective vehicle?" Starling laughed, thankful for the interruption before his own bad memories took hold.

"Sure, it's the newest thing," Lovett answered. "It still needs a little work because there's a nut loose behind the wheel."

"And you're about as funny as screen doors on a submarine," Gillam replied.

Curtis liked them right away. They reminded him of Abbot and Costello routines he saw on the old television shows his aunt liked to watch.

"Larry, Sam, this is Curtis Harris. Curtis is the one who discovered the ah, situation here at the house. He's the one who called me."

Both detectives came forward and shook Curtis' hand.

"Thank you," said Gillam. "That was very brave of you. Most people would just run away and not get involved. Even adults."

"That's right," interjected Sam. "I bet you were with some friends who didn't want to call. I bet they were even more scared than you were."

"I was plenty scared. They didn't know what was going on. They never even went in the house they were too scared."

Sam's attempt to draw out some information worked, but then it didn't look like it was information they could use. No one else went inside.

"Do you mind showing us exactly what you did?" Sam continued.

Curtis looked up at John and getting a wink and a nod

from him felt more comfortable and confident. "Sure. Come on."

After Gillam and Lovett retrieved flashlights from Gillam's car, Curtis took them to the door where he squeezed through the plywood board. There was no need to squeeze through now. The door had been removed for the investigation and to remove the body. It was just lying up against the doorway now.

Gillam moved the plywood barricade and placed it against the house. The house still had a lingering foul odor, but there were other smells, familiar smells. They followed Curtis who was now inching forward into the house, following the path he took only yesterday morning. Curtis was shaking. He almost jumped when John put his hand on his shoulder, but it soon turned out to have a calming effect, and the boy continued through the house.

They came to the room where the body was found. Of course, there was nothing there now. The window was still unblocked, but framed with the yellow crime scene tape going from corner to corner making a big 'X'.

The floor was clean. There wasn't a spot of dirt, much less blood anywhere to be found. That was the other smell; chemicals. Someone came in after the initial investigation and cleaned the room.

"John, did you have someone clean this area?"

"Not me. We don't clean crime scenes. Somebody, without permission, came behind us and did this. Someone's covering their tracks."

"The tracks already got covered once. Now they have literally been removed. We were hoping there would be traces of blood still here to get another sample."

"Curtis, what happened to you in this room?"

"It was dark in here and I couldn't see. I tripped and fell, and thought I got red paint on my hands. I tried to rub it off on my pants at first and then I went over to the board on the window and I pushed it out. That's when I seen, I mean, that's when I saw the man on the floor and the blood on my hands. I ran outside and my friends came running up and helped me."

"Curtis, you wiped your hands on your pants. Do you still have those pants at your house?" Gillam asked, with anticipation and hope.

"Yes. My Aunt Dorothy washed them. They smelled bad, but they weren't torn or anything and I can still wear them. She cleaned my shoes too."

Gillam's shoulders sank. "Did any of your friends get blood on them?" He was grasping for straws now.

"No."

"Well, that's that then," Lovett said.

"But James let me use his handkerchief to wipe the blood off my hands."

All the detectives looked at the boy. It was John who spoke first.

"Curtis, what did you do with the handkerchief after you

wiped the blood off?"

"I tried to give it back to James, but he wouldn't take it. I don't blame him none. It had blood all on it and it smelled bad too."

"Okay. And what did you do with it then?"

"I threw it away."

Another let down. There was almost no way for them to find it now. And even if they did, it may have been contaminated with other trash and who knows what.

John gave it one more try. "Curtis, can you tell us where you threw it away?"

Curtis went to the open window. He pointed out towards the woods. "There," he said continuing to point.

Gillam was the first to see the white speck in the bushes.

Curtis led them outside and over to the bushes which lined the woods. There in one of the bushes was a white handkerchief with what appeared to be dried bloodstains. Gillam took it out of the bush.

"That's it," Curtis said. "I didn't want to touch it anymore and I sure wasn't going to put it in my pocket, so I just threw it here. I'm sorry. I know it's littering. I wasn't thinking at the time."

"And a small child shall lead them," John said. "Curtis, again you came through."

Curtis brandished a big grin on his face, but he wasn't sure why. Everyone appeared to be happy and was praising him.

He was glad they weren't mad at him for littering.

Gillam and Lovett left heading for the Medical Examiner's office to deliver the handkerchief and the bullet to Doctor Higdon. They were sure to check to see if there were any cars, vans, motorcycles, or even stray dogs watching them. Things were getting to the point where they wondered if there might even be a satellite trained on them.

Starling and Curtis went back to the car and John drove over to an adjoining street as directed by Curtis where they parked. Curtis led him into the woods a short distance and there the 'fort' stood. It was just as John imagined it to be.

"Be careful. We have booby-traps set up," Curtis advised.

John looked and saw strings tied between trees near the ground. These led to some rusted tin cans which would make noise when disturbed. Almost like an early warning system he used in the army. Only no flares would go off and no machine-guns would start firing. At least he hoped not.

They got to what would be considered a front entrance and John saw there was a large chain wrapped around a tree and through a door where there used to be a door knob. There was a big lock keeping the chain secure. It didn't matter you could get in from just about anywhere else if you wanted to.

Curtis dug into his pocket, pulled out a key, unlocked the lock, and told John to come in. The inside of the fort was warm, moist and there was a smell reminding him of how he would dig for worms before going fishing.

The fort needed some major renovations. He knew the boys thought it was great. He wasn't about to burst Curtis' bubble on how shabby it really was. But he wasn't going to pass it for inspection. Not yet.

"Well Curtis, I see you and the others have done a lot of work here, but there needs to be a lot more done before I can give it my Okay. First, who owns this property? Did they give you permission to build the fort here?"

"Nobody owns it. It's just some woods. There ain't no house or any signs anywhere."

"You meant to say there's not a house here?" John looked at him.

"Yes sir. Sorry." Curtis apologized. "There is not a house here."

"That's better. Even though there is not a house here, it doesn't mean the property is not owned by someone. All land is owned by someone; a person, a company, the city, or some other government agency. There isn't a piece of property which doesn't have an owner. And property owners are careful about who they let on their property. If someone comes on their property, even without permission, and gets hurt, they can sue the landowner. The landowner can have trespassers arrested. So you see, it's important to find out who the landowner is and get written permission to be on their property. Making sure both you and the land owner are protected."

"Does that mean we got to take the fort down?"

"Not necessarily. We just need to find out who the owner is and then go from there."

"How do you find out who the owner is?"

"I can do it by checking records at the county office. They have records about who owns property in the whole county."

"You can do that? Would you? Please?"

"Oh, all right," he said, with mock annoyance, "but not today. Maybe I can find out on Monday."

John was almost knocked over when the boy rushed him and gave him a hug. He held the boy a minute and patted him on the shoulder.

"I've got to get you back. Your Aunt Dorothy won't like it if I keep you out too long." He thought his voice may have cracked a little and hoped the boy didn't notice.

After dropping Curtis off at his house and getting a chance to see Dorothy again, John called Tommy to see if there was any information for him. Tommy told him about his computer guy hacking the system for a second. Long enough to get the face page for something called *Operation Back Street* and some government agencies which appeared to be associated with it. Starling stated he never heard of anything like it and wondered why the agencies on the list were being so secret.

Tommy apologized for not having any information on the

black car and van, but said they would keep trying. Tommy also asked if they found anything useful. Starling filled him in with as much information as he knew. He didn't go into any detail about Aunt Dorothy though.

Starling called Gillam. They were still on the way to the Medical Examiner's office when he answered. He told him it was a no-go so far on the check for the car and van, but gave him what McGill said about the computer site.

"I've never heard of any such animal," Gillam said. Of course, they could have hundreds of 'operations' which we know nothing about. Maybe thousands."

Lovett, who was listening in on Gillam's phone speaker said, "It can't be good if the military and the CDC are in it together. But why Homeland Security and the DoJ? Maybe it's another Roswell."

"Roswell?" Starling inquired.

"You know. Where they captured the UFO that crashed in the desert; in what, the fifties?"

"It was in July, 1947," Gillam corrected. "Just outside of Roswell, New Mexico."

"Yeah, I should have known you'd know that."

"Well, something's going on and they're taking a lot of steps to keep things quiet," Starling said.

"You think they may be involved with Kim's death and all the other stuff going on?" Lovett asked.

"It's hard to say. There's not enough information yet.

Another reason why we've got to keep digging."

"I just hope we're not digging our own graves," Lovett said.

There was silent agreement from everyone.

CHAPTER 28

Azira wanted to find out more about *Operation Back Street* and try to get the information on the vehicles for Tommy. But what really bothered him and what he really wanted to know was who was behind their computer security.

Could it be someone he knew or someone he worked with? He doubted it. No one was close to that level of skill. There may have only been a hand full of people able to keep him out of a system when he wanted to get in. One or two of them were in prison. One was out of prison, but not allowed anywhere near a computer (yeah, right), or faced going back. Everyone else was out of country, working for some big company, or part of the government.

He wanted to find out. He needed to find out. He had a reputation to uphold. Not to mention his pride.

Jenny, for the first time in her young life, outside of her family, needed help; real help, possibly lifesaving help. She was stuck. She didn't have access to family, friends, or even the law. She was confined to a building with no windows; at least not in her room, the cafeteria, or the computer control room where she spent most of her day. It may have been underground as far as she knew.

She didn't have any friends, and there was no one to talk to except others who worked in the same areas she did and they were like robots. Lacking personality, not very friendly, and talking only about work related things. Not even weather or sports, and certainly not any of what was really going on in The Facility.

She was allowed access to the computers, but it was monitored and she was watched. She didn't have the clearance to get into certain sites where she could find the information she wanted. She knew she could get in; however, she wasn't sure what would happen to her if she did and got caught. It was a decision she juggled with from time to time.

She was allowed to play games on her computer for entertainment and to pass the time. Sites the general needed to approve. One of the games she was allowed access to was one she had invented. This was information unknown to the general and she wasn't about to tell him either.

Jenny wondered about the hacker who got around her first line of security. They were good. They, he, she, whomever, it didn't much matter. She hoped they would try again. It was the first real test since she was given the responsibility. It gave her something to look forward to. She might even be able to make contact. As long as it was a hacker with her skill. If it was, she might be able to formulate a plan to make contact without anyone ever knowing. Maybe she found the help she needed.

Azira got in touch with several of his usual computer buddies. A video conference call was set up and he inquired about who was the best computer black-hat jammer out there, not in prison or overseas. Someone who might even be working for the government.

Several names came up and several arguments broke out about the abilities of some of the names mentioned. One of his friends even suggested that Azira was the best and wondered if this was a test. He assured the others that he was not the subject of his own search. He might have an ego, but it didn't go that far. Finally, there was an agreement of sorts. A short list was made; however, nobody on it stood out.

"Is there anyone who has gone off radar lately?" Azira asked. "Someone who suddenly disappeared from the sites?"

One of the faces on a computer screen spoke up. "I just remembered. There's this girl, new, but brilliant. She calls herself *Wonder Woman*. She's the one who invented the online game 'Evil Tempest' before some company bought it up, added a lot of graphics and changed its name. There's a story she got busted by the Feds for some bank fraud or something and she went dark. There are other rumors she may have gone underground. I'm not sure of the whole story, but no one has heard from her in a while. I think she lived right there in your area too."

Azira laughed. "One of the companies I contract with

bought that game. I played the game online before the company refined it. I recall playing against *Wonder Woman*. No wonder I couldn't beat her. It was one of the few games I wasn't number one on. Could she be the one I'm looking for? Is she savvy enough to be a jammer?"

"She's as good as any on the list and better than most," another one of the talking heads on a screen said. "I also hear she's hot."

"Okay guys, thanks for the help. I'll check into this and see where it goes. If you hear anything, you know where to find me."

"Do you need any help trying to get back into their system?" asked a head.

"No, not right now, but I'll let you know if I do. I want to take this slow and not set off a bunch of bells and whistles. I think there might be more to this than meets the eye."

Azira got into the mainframe of the software gaming company which bought the online version of *Evil Tempest*. There must be some legal documents on file if they purchased the game directly from her.

He didn't need to hack into the files. He used his password from the company to access the correct directory. *Almost like cheating*, he thought. He found the files easily enough.

She was underage at the time of the purchase, so the transaction included her parents. All the information was there.

The date, the amount, her name, birth date, and address. *"Hello, Jenny Jordan, aka Wonder Woman,"* he said, out loud. "Why did you disappear and what are you doing with those government blowhards?"

The next thing Azira did was to access the public information section of the Fulton County District Attorney's Office to check for criminal records. Nothing.

"Okay," he said to no one, "no arrest record there. Not if it was squashed. Not if some deal was made. Maybe they made a federal case out of it."

He then got into an FBI data bank, one he set up with a back door for himself just before he left. He managed to maneuver thorough several sites to get to files from the United States District Court for Northern Georgia. There he found a search warrant issued by a Federal Judge for her address.

"Bingo!"

The search warrant was for computers and files among other things. Still there was no arrest disposition. No court record.

He was positive now some deal had been made. Some deal she did not want to volunteer to be a part of, but didn't have a choice. Or at least, not knowing the full details of what it was she was getting into. He was now determined more than ever to make contact with her. But how?

William N. Gilmore

CHAPTER 29

There were no cars or vans following them this trip. They were sure of it. Gillam and Lovett kept a close watch on all vehicles no matter what color they were. They got to the Medical Examiner's office with no incidents. Gillam was about to ring the buzzer when Lovett checked the front door. It was unlocked. They weren't sure what to think now. Was it left purposely unlocked or was someone there who didn't belong.

They proceeded with caution. They moved quietly as they had at the property section. Moving up and checking open doors. They heard some noise coming from one of the examining rooms and both drew their weapons. They both entered the room. Gillam going high and Lovett going low. They both held a bead on the man with his back to them.

Doctor Higdon turned from the body on the table and was holding someone's brain in his hands. He looked surprised, but not as surprised as the two detectives. "Well, do you want me to drop it or raise my hands and let it drip all over me?" The doctor asked.

If the past couple of days hadn't been so extreme, the situation may have actually been funny.

"We're sorry, Doctor Higdon," they said putting their guns away. "We didn't know if there may be trouble in here,"

Gillam continued. "The front door was unlocked."

"Of course, it was unlocked. This is still a government building. We still have business going on. This poor bastard died very quickly when he stepped in front of a MARTA bus. You want some local veterinarian doing this autopsy? When they bring me some business am I supposed to say, 'Oops, sorry, I need to take a break this week.' Of course, not."

"Here son, you want to help?" holding the brain out towards Lovett. It was still dripping and the doctor's gloves were covered with blood and ..., other stuff.

Lovett, usually strong stomached, gave a heave or two and ran out of the room. He barely got past Jaccob who was entering. You could hear the footfalls as he ran towards the restroom. Everyone hoped he would make it. None more than Lovett.

After Gillam got through laughing, he told Doctor Higdon they would wait for him in the conference room. The doctor agreed and told him it would be about twenty or thirty minutes.

After about ten minutes, Lovett walked into the conference room. He held a wet paper towel over his mouth.

"Do you have any gum, a mint, anything? I've got this bad taste in my mouth still."

"No, sorry. Did you make it?"

"Just barely. Since we missed lunch, I didn't have much and it was mostly dry heaves. Now I've got that burning in my throat and the bad taste it gives you."

"You're right. We did miss lunch. That's a rarity. Good thing for you though. If you're hungry now though—"

"No, thank you! You'll have a lot more than spilled coffee in your lap."

"And just what exactly would your face be doing in my lap?"

"Just shut up. I don't want to hear your voice for a while." Sam sat down, put his head back, his feet up and put the paper towel over his eyes.

Before Sam had a chance to relax, Doctor Higdon came in. He gave a disapproving look at Lovett. "Jaccob is finishing up with the gentleman; what have you got for me?"

Lovett did not sit up. He didn't even remove the paper towel.

Gillam pulled from his pocket a small, plastic, zip-locked bag. Inside the bag was the business end of a 9mm bullet. He pulled another package out and this was a small paper bag. He opened the bag and showed Doctor Higdon a blood-dried handkerchief.

"Lovett found the slug in the dash of your wagon at the impound yard and the handkerchief came from outside the abandoned house on Griffin Street. The young boy who found the dead man and got his blood on his hands wiped his hands on the handkerchief and threw it in the bushes. Is there anything we can do with these?

"Gentleman," the doctor began, "we're in business."

Gillam smiled.

Lovett moaned.

CHAPTER 30

General Cunningham called in one of his aids. An officer who never smiled, never questioned an order, and never let the general down.

"Where are we on the police lieutenant and the rest of the situations?"

"He's an idiot, sir, but he's our idiot, at least for now," the aid said in a true southern drawl. "We have him by the short hairs and he'll do whatever we tell him. He likes getting paid and he likes to breathe even more. We have a team keeping tabs on him just in case."

"Where did he get the idea we wanted him to take out the Assistant Medical Examiner and torch his office? He just put a spotlight on the situation. That's something we don't need."

"Exactly what I mean, he's an idiot. He took it upon himself to do it. He didn't think there was any other way at the time. He overreacted. He attempted to cover his tracks on the Assistant Medical Examiner when he recovered the body of the bum. It's still listed as an accident and there's nothing in the report about any other body. Right now, it's not an issue with the department. He did get the body of the whore out along with all the records. The incendiary device he set at the ME's office somehow failed, but there's no way to trace it. It was a simple homemade device. This also appears to have not been reported. Those two Narcotics Detectives are scratching their heads and although they know something is going on, they have no clue. The lieutenant is holding onto their reins."

"What about the team we sent over to help him tie up some of the loose ends?" the general asked.

"They recovered all the evidence from the Police Department and the Crime Lab without incident and did a cleanup of the house where the bum died. They took control of the bodies of the whore and the bum and they have been disposed of in the usual manner."

"Good," said the general, "were there any problems?"

"Just a few minor hiccups. One agent assigned to the team is being reassigned because he may have been compromised. He'll be replaced unless you think other action is necessary. The GPS unit is stationary at the police department; it may have been found. There's nothing on it or in it to show its origin. The two detectives have no idea who was following them. They appear to be receiving some assistance from other members of the department and possibly outside agencies. It doesn't appear to be a factor at this time."

"Keep me advised," the general stated.

"Yes sir. Also, the missing wrecker driver appears to be a coincidence or possibly a random act such as a carjacking. He's still missing and there's been no further evidence of him anywhere. He may be in the river or rotting somewhere. He has no connection to anything except picking up the wrecked wagon and dropping it off. The police lieutenant assures us there is no other evidence. Nothing which would trace back to us."

"What about our internal security?"

"Attempts were made on the computer to identify the vehicles, but the registration for our vehicles is blocked. An attempt was made to hack the main frame; however, Ms. Jordan was able to stop the intruder. The hacker has not been able to be identified yet, nor where it originated. There does not appear to be any leak or security breach in the computers or the operators, to include Ms. Jordan. No other attempts have been made."

"Do you think we still need the police lieutenant?" The general asked.

"He's a screw up, sir and I think things would run smoother if he wasn't in the picture sometimes, but then again, we may still need his ability to get certain things done in the police department, at least for now. Then we can use him as a fall guy or just have him take a trip. The others can be taken care of later. Too much scrutiny will be made if they disappear or have an accident now. Disposing of cops is touchy."

"Are we sure the wrecker driver is no problem?" The general asked. "I don't believe in coincidences. Especially if it's connected in any way with the operation."

"Yes sir, I'll make sure of it myself," the aid stated.

"Have the compromised agent reassigned. For now, anyway. We need to wrap up all these loose ends. We cannot let a couple of bozo's ruin everything we have worked so hard on."

"And the rest of the operation, sir? The real operation that is; do you think any of them would understand?"

"We are the real operation," the general said, as he stood. "It might not be what is on the mission statement and it may not be what the politicians have in mind, but it is what this country needs. I am trying to save this country, son, and by God, I will do it if I have to shove it down their throats. And they will thank me for it someday. Just like in war, there are casualties and acceptable losses. There is collateral damage and unspeakable things done to win. However, there are heroes too; those who must make sacrifices for the better good. Which is why we are here. This is a war and we are fighting a battle to win our country back. I hate having to go behind the backs of our leaders, but they have gotten soft. We must stand up. We must be the heroes. You *are* with me are you not, son?"

"Yes, sir!"

"Good. Now get me the report on the latest production numbers and the quality of the product. There is going to be a meeting of lab supervisors in the morning and I want to see if they are meeting the standards we want."

"Yes sir," the aid said. "Also, there's one thing if you don't mind. I have tickets for a ballgame on Sunday. I was wondering if you might want to get out of here for a while. You keep yourself cooped up and I don't think I've seen you even leave The Facility for weeks."

"Thank you, but I have too much on my mind and things to do. You go ahead. You haven't had a day to yourself either. I have been running you pretty hard. Go. Enjoy yourself. Maybe you will meet a young lady. You do not want to get yourself stuck with an old fart like me this weekend."

"Sir, you may need me. I don't mind. Besides, I should follow-up on some of those things we talked about."

"You can take care of those things first and then the rest of the weekend is yours. That is an order," the general smiled.

"Yes sir. I'll get those reports you wanted right away."

He liked this kid. He even presented him a special Cold War style spy watch for his birthday. Loyal, dedicated, and he had a head on his shoulders. If things turned out as he hoped, he would go far. If not, he could not go far enough.

William N. Gilmore

CHAPTER 31

Azira came up with an idea. If his timing was wrong or if he got discovered, he didn't know if he would be able to try again. He didn't know if he might put someone else in jeopardy and if that someone might be Jenny Jordan. He still was only about ninety percent sure she was the one to block his entry into the secret mainframe. Everything so far, seemed to point in that direction.

He set up as many safeguards as he could think of to keep from being found out; from being backtracked. He purchased a "disposable" laptop from a pawnshop with one of his many fake ID's. One he could just walk away from if his attempts failed or if he believed he became compromised.

There was still the possibility he was wrong not just about whom was at the computer, but what their intentions might be. He needed to find out. He knew they would have set up new programs to keep him out. New security measures he might not be able to get around. So, he would have to try a different backdoor. One they wouldn't have thought of. A backdoor only one person might be able to understand.

"Here goes nothing," he said, and added a little prayer to the computer gods and the gods of chance as his fingers flew.

He opened the site he needed. *Evil Tempest* flashed in

brilliant colors on his screen. It wasn't the software company's version. It was the original, on-line version created by *Wonder Woman*. It wasn't available to everyone. The software company removed the game from the web when it bought it, but there were still some secret sites where the game was available.

He was sure there were backdoors left by her. As he well knew, all game creators possessed their own cheats and hidden areas within their sites. He was hoping he could find one of those hidden sites. One she would have accessed recently.

He put his screen name, *Magician*, in the player name box and selected one player mode. He worked his way through the game and looked for things which would be easy for others to miss. He went through the game several times. If she accessed the game, hopefully the same computer she was able to use to block him, there would be electronic fingerprints which he would be able to backtrack to her. He would essentially be hacking her computer from her own computer.

He worked on the task for several hours. He didn't think it would be easy, but he thought he would have had at least something to show for his effort by now. She hid things deep. *Or maybe*, he thought, *she hid things right in plain sight*. He started over. He went to the player name box and put in *Wonder Woman*. Nothing. Too easy. He tried several names including hers. Still nothing. He didn't think it would be a common name. Too easy for an accidental entry. Maybe some word play. He began trying palindromes and anagrams.

When he typed in Tempest Live and hit enter, a whole new screen popped up.

"What the—"

It appeared to be a journal of sorts. It was an account of how she ended up at a secret government facility. A location she had no idea about because she was not allowed outside. She believed it was underground. She worked for some general who oversaw the operation. She was supposed to work for him for three months and she would be released. Now it was four months later. She believed she was a prisoner there and would never be allowed to leave.

If he didn't know better with all the things going on, he would have thought this was a new story line for a game or an outline for a book.

He saw something which gave him hope. The last passage was just entered yesterday. The diary was still active and she visited it regularly. He would leave her a message and hope she got it very soon instead of trying to access the secret main frame again.

He hadn't realized it for a few minutes, but he was getting mad. He was mad she was being told lies. He was mad the government, our government, had in effect, kidnapped her and was holding her prisoner. He was mad there were secret operations his tax dollars paid for which conducted themselves in this manner. He was mad that for right now, he couldn't do much to help her. That one thing was something he could change. And it started right here, right now.

Jenny, I am someone who can help. We met playing your game and again today. I have friends who want to find out what is going on there and help get you out. Can you help us help you? Leave message here. The Magician.

He didn't know how soon she would get back on her site. Obviously, it wasn't something they knew about. He hoped she would remember him. He hoped she would respond. There was the possibility she would be too scared to do anything more once she found out someone knew about and hacked into her private site. It was a gamble, nonetheless, it was one which needed to be made.

He had been at this for a while. He was tired. He powered down most of his equipment and headed for bed. He would call Tommy first thing.

Jenny was at her terminal. It was Friday and most of the usual crew would disappear for the weekend. She didn't know if they went to homes, barracks, or sleep chambers to be wakened for duty on Monday morning. The weekend crew was just as exciting as the others.

She read books and magazines; listened to music, and played brain games to keep her occupied. There was no outside contact; no television, no radio, and no newspapers. There was a small gym with exercise equipment she sometimes used. There were even tanning beds. The food in the cafeteria wasn't too bad

All this reminded her of some science fiction movie about being on a space ship or in a bunker as a survivor of a nuclear holocaust. She spent most of her time in her quarters. A small room reminding her of a hospital room with almost the same smell. It was no wonder she spent most of the time in the room crying.

She was allowed limited web access on her computer for work related items. Sites needed to be approved by the general. She was monitored and watched around the clock. Either by the security personnel stationed all over the place or by one of the dozens of cameras which were always spying. There were so many restrictions on the computer access she had, it was a wonder she could get any work done. It wasn't just a prison, it was Hell.

Some of the sites approved by the general were game sites. When she decided to play a game, it was usually something which would test her brain. She liked the intellectual games. But occasionally, she liked to dumb down a little and play something where she could be the super hero, the savior of humanity, or maybe even the villain. Those were some of the choices her game, *Evil Tempest* gave. She accessed the game site and before she went on to play, she wanted to add some to her secret diary. She looked around discreetly to make sure no one was watching her too closely right then. She typed in her secret password and opened the diary site.

Jenny stared at the screen for a second and literally

jumped back. One of the techs asked her what happened. One of the security guards started walking towards her. She quickly closed the site with the slap of one button on her keyboard.

"Yuck," she said. "Did you see that spider? It was huge."

The security guard laughed at her and returned to his post.

"Oh, I hate spiders too," said the tech. "You killed it, didn't you? It didn't come over here, did it?" she asked, scooting away in her chair.

"I got it I think. I'm going to the restroom to wash my hands," she said holding her hand out.

"Keep that nasty stuff away from me," the tech said, scooting even further away as Jenny passed her.

Jenny got to the restroom and went to the sink. She ran the cold water, but not to wash her hands. She scoped up water, bent over and buried her face in her hands. The cold water was a welcomed relief. *Did I really see that? Could I be cracking up?* She silently asked herself.

She rose and looked in the mirror. Water was dripping down her face, mixed in with tears, but it couldn't wash away the smile.

She composed herself as much as possible and hoped her nervousness did not show through. She left the restroom, walking up the hallway with a little more confidence in her step. The security guard smiled at her as she passed.

She returned to her station with some paper towels and

pretended to clean up around her keyboard, making remarks about how gooey it was. The other tech, having a queasy look, refused to watch her wipe up the invisible spider guts. She averted her eyes when Jenny put the wadded-up paper towel, sure to hold the spider innards, next to her own keyboard. Just as Jenny hoped.

Jenny made it back to her hidden site without being noticed and verified she had not been seeing things. *The Magician.* Was this the attempted hacker from earlier? The name rang a bell. He said he had played her game. She remembered him now. A very skilled player. One of the best. If she had not used some of her own programmed cheats, he would have beaten her at her own game. But could he be trusted? Could this be a test by the general? She may have just been given the chance she was praying for.

Now it would be up to her to take the next step. Was she up to it? There was only one way to find out. She typed out one word. One word only which might start something once it began, it could not be stopped.

Yes.

William N. Gilmore

CHAPTER 32

Gillam dropped Lovett off at his car in the department parking lot. Sam made sure there were no devices of any kind on, in, or around his car before getting in it for the drive home.

"Call me when you get home," Lovett said, through the driver's window. "I just want to make sure you get there without any problems."

"See, I knew you really cared. What are you going to tell Debbie?"

"That we're running away together. What do you think?"

"No, idiot, about what's been going on. Are you still going to have her go to her mother's?"

"I don't know," Sam sighed. "I think I'll leave it up to her. She's a strong-willed woman. A fighter. She doesn't scare easily and I wouldn't be a bit surprised if she didn't strap on one of her guns and want to come out with us."

"Hey, we could use the back-up. Did you say, *her* guns? Do you think that's smart having a woman in the house with her own guns?"

"She's the daughter of a cop, the wife of a cop, and besides you, there's no one else I'd rather have my back. Or my front."

Gillam laughed. "Okay, I'll call you. Don't forget to ask

Deb about going to the game on Sunday."

"I already did. You have a date with a pretty redheaded lady who won't cough up fur balls."

"I could make a comment about that, but I won't."

"Thanks. I did leave myself wide open. I'll see you later, partner. Be careful," Sam said, waving out the window as he began to drive off.

"You bet," Gillam yelled at him. *You too, my friend.*

Gillam made the drive home without seeing anything which appeared to be following him. It was already dusk with most of the sun dipping below the horizon. The clouds were all the pastel colors. Mostly reds.

He hoped things were quieting down some from the hectic few days. This weekend would be a nice change. Rest, a date, a ballgame, a date, maybe some football. He was going on a date. *Yep, that was a change all right,* he thought. He was thinking about the redhead when he pulled into his apartment complex and parked. *I hope she doesn't smoke,* he continued his thoughts, as he walked to his door. He put the key in the lock and opened the door when he felt the blow to his head.

A split second of intense pain followed by fireworks of bright stars, soon faded into what must have been the blackness of space. It took the place of the more enjoyable thoughts of Gillam as he fell through the doorway and into his own apartment.

Lovett called his wife to let her know he was on the way. Something they both did for each other so they would have a pretty good idea who was coming through the door. He told her he would be there in about twenty minutes. She was cooking dinner.

Sam arrived home without incident and without being followed. He entered the house and called out "It's me." There was no answer. "Deb, I'm home." Again, no answer. He went into the living room. The television was on. He could smell the aroma of the cooking. Again, he yelled out. This time a lot louder. "Debbie." There was no answer and his heart went into his throat. He started to pull his weapon when the back door opened and his dog, Stella, came running up and jumped on him.

"Well, it's about time you got your sorry ass home, old man," Debbie said, closing the back door behind her. She saw the look on Sam's face and knew things were just not right. She locked the door and walked over to him. "Sam, what is it? Is everything all right?"

"It is now," he said, swallowing hard. He grabbed her and hugged her, bringing her close to him, not wanting to let her go.

"Well, this is nice," she said, but still guarded. She repeated once more, "Sweetheart, is everything all right?"

"It's been one of those days," he said, giving them some space so he could look into her eyes. "And when you didn't answer when I came in, I was just thinking something bad was going on."

"Sam, I've seen this before. I know there's something going on and I also know you're going to tell me. Why don't you get comfortable and I'll get dinner ready. Then we'll talk. Okay, sweetie."

"Sounds like a plan to me. You're a jewel. Did Larry call?"

"No. Was he supposed to?"

"Yeah. When he got home. He should have been there by now."

"Well, maybe he stopped at a store or something on the way."

"You're probably right."

Gillam felt the Big Bang going through his head. He tried to open his eyes, but all he saw at first was the sun. It swallowed the whole sky. Nothing else was visible. It wasn't hot like he thought it would be; however, the light gave him the worst headache he ever experienced. Even worse than the time he did a header on his bicycle at the basketball court trying to impress Sherry Abbott.

It seemed he could reach out and touch it; he wanted to. He tried to move his hands, but for some reason they were behind him and his arms wouldn't move. He struggled a bit and then realized he was tied up. So were his feet.

The sun, shrinking slowly as he watched, was about the

size of an orange now, the whole universe behind it black, without stars. As it became the size of a marble, everything began to fade a little into an unfocused cloud. The headache remained as the edges of the cloud seemed to lighten as it shrank, allowing a picture to form on the outer edges. After a few seconds, some normal vision began to return; however, his perception of what he saw was off.

He could tell he was on the floor; the floor of his own apartment. He didn't know how long he may have been there. As his vision cleared, he could see a set of big boots. He thought; *my boots are in the closet, aren't they? Did Cali drag them out? Puss and boots, puss and boots.* He almost laughed, but he thought he might throw up instead. Cali was probably hiding somewhere anyway.

"I'm sorry I hit you so hard mister," a voice said. "I thought I done killed you."

"You mean I'm not dead?" Gillam said, a little of reality setting in.

"Not yet. Not unless you tell me what's going on."

Gillam still a bit groggy didn't know how long he had been unconscious. He knew he needed to stall. As long as he was talking, he was alive. Alive was a good thing.

"Then I'm not going to tell you what's going on, even if I knew what the hell it is you're talking about."

"What?" asked the unfamiliar voice.

Gillam spoke very slowly, pausing as much as he could,

273

dragging it out. He knew he must keep the conversation going."

"You said you wouldn't kill me unless I told you what was going on. So, if I tell you what's going on, then you'll kill me."

"What? No. That's not what I meant. I mean if you don't tell me what's going on, *then* I'll kill you."

"Oh, okay, I think I get it. If I don't tell you what I know, you'll kill me. Do I have it right, now?" He tried to look up, but still couldn't focus on much.

"Yeah, yeah, that's it."

"Okay, so even if I know something I won't be able to tell you because I'll be dead."

"You're trying to confuse me."

"Confuse *you*? I think you're *already* confused. Do you have the right address? Are you sure you have the right guy?"

"Yeah, you're the right guy."

"Okay, I give up. I'm sorry. I swear I didn't know she was married. She said she was divorced."

"Who did?"

"The woman I slept with. She was your wife, right?"

"What the hell are you talking about, mister?"

"Okay, I confess. I'm having an affair with your wife. It's been going on for months. We were going to run away together. We're in love. We can't deny it any longer."

"What are you getting at, mister? I'm not even married."

"Well, who was that woman?"

"What woman? I think I hit you pretty hard mister. Maybe I did more damage than I thought. I'm not here because of my wife. Wait, I mean, I don't have no wife. I'm not here because of nobody's wife."

"Oh God, don't tell me she was your mother."

"My *mother?* My mother is in a nursing home. You're treading on some dangerous ground there mister."

"I'm *lying* on the ground, you idiot. Okay, maybe it was your sister, your aunt, maybe even your second cousin twice removed. I don't know. And to tell the truth I don't care. We're still in love and we're—"

The front door burst open and Sam leapt into the front room as Debbie went down on one knee behind the doorframe. Both held big semi-autos with laser pointers. Two red dots appeared on the forehead of the big man sitting in the chair. He was lucky he was only holding a tire iron which he dropped immediately without even being told.

Maybe he wasn't quite a dumb as he seemed, thought Gillam, *but then again, maybe he was.*

"Is he alone?" Lovett asked, scanning the apartment.

"As far as I know. I didn't see anyone else." *Or at least any other shoes while I was on the floor,* he thought.

"What took you so long?" Gillam asked, as Debbie tried to untie the duct tape binding his hands.

"I was hungry and stopped for some fries," Lovett said, keeping a bead on the man. "Who's your friend here?"

"I don't know," Larry said. "We were just getting to that. I did find out he's not married. I kept him talking for a while. I didn't know how long I was out. I knew if I didn't call, you'd show up. I just hoped it would be in time."

"That's what good partners and their wives with big guns are for." Sam said.

"Now all I have to do is find a *good* partner," Larry said, as he got his hands free and began removing the tape from his feet. "You available Deb, I like your style and you're prettier too."

She winked at Sam, "I might be easy, but I'm not cheap. I'm high maintenance, only the best for me; in my man and my guns. I think I better stick with what I know for now, but keep the offer warm just in case."

Gillam got to his feet a little wobbly. Debbie helped him keep steady. He removed the rest of the tape from his wrists, pulling some hairs out. Now he knew how Peterson felt. He *had* to use the sticky stuff. The bastard.

"Okay friend, let's have your story. First, who are you?"

"That laser is boring a hole in my head. I can feel it. Can you point it somewheres else?"

"Sure," Lovett said. "How's that?" pointing it right between a large set of man boobs.

"I'm nobody," he said, speaking now with difficulty. He began to cry. He put his face in his big meaty hands and bawled like a baby. He was shaking all over. Maybe, more like bouncing. He was saying something; however, it was unintelligible through the sobs and the big hands.

Debbie got Larry over to a couch and he sat down facing the big guy. She went into the kitchen and returned with a wet cloth for him and one for his attacker. Still no one knew for sure what was going on.

"Okay, let's try this again," Gillam began. "Calm down and tell us who you are, and why the hell you tried to kill me?"

The big guy took a couple of gasps and sniffled several more. He blew into the cloth and started off slowly. "I didn't try to kill you, honest, I'm not like that. I just wanted to make sure you weren't going to hurt me."

"Hurt *you?* I don't keep a bulldozer in this small apartment, so how could I hurt you?"

"I thought you might shoot me or something."

"Well now that you bring it up," Gillam looked over at Lovett and winked. "Sam, shoot him."

The man's eyes opened wide and then he put his big arms up over his face. It wouldn't have mattered because Sam was still aiming at the middle of the man's massive chest.

"Okay, okay, we won't shoot you," Gillam said, almost feeling bad; almost. The big guy seemed to be a can or two short of a six pack. "I'll give you one more chance," nodding over to Sam. "Who are you?"

"I'm Bubba Thompson," he said with a heavy sigh, peeking between the massive arms. "I drive a wrecker."

Gillam knew his head was hurting. He wondered if the guy was right and he was hurt more than he thought. He shook his head; the wrong thing to do; he almost passed out again. The dark cloud slowly passed and he finally said, "Did you say you're Thompson? Everyone thinks *you're* the dead one."

"I had to do it. I hated putting the wrecker in the river, but I couldn't think of nothing else. I had to make folks think I was drowned. I was afraid I'd get killed next."

"Put your arms down and tell us *who* would kill *you,* and what do you mean *next?*" Lovett asked the question this time.

Bubba slowly put his arms in his lap. "The same guy that killed the guy in the meat wagon. You know, the one I picked up and dropped off at the impound yard."

"Are you talking about the Medical Examiner's wagon?"

"That's what I said."

"What makes you think the guy in the meat wagon was killed?" Gillam returned, wishing he hadn't spoken at all.

"I saw it. I wasn't supposed to be there, it was wrong, I know it, but there I was and I saw it."

All the pain, all the clouds, and all the stars went away from Gillam's head for the moment.

"What did you see Bubba? Tell us everything you saw."

CHAPTER 33

Tommy McGill answered his phone on the third ring. It was his buddy Azira.

"I've made contact," the kid almost shouted.

"With aliens?" Tommy guessed.

"No, with a girl."

"Well, that's just grand, Azira. I hope you live happily ever after. When's the wedding?" Tommy laughed.

"No. At *Operation Back Street*."

Tommy didn't have a response for a moment.

"Tommy, did you hear me? I made contact."

"What does that mean?" he asked, sounding a lot more serious. "Did you get the bloody info on the car and van?"

Azira laughed himself. "No. I found the girl who put up the computer security for them. I made contact with her through her game."

"Okay, Azira. Start from the beginning and tell me the whole grand story. Don't make a hash of it and have me to ask a bunch of silly questions now. Fill in everything like you're writing a program code."

It took about fifteen minutes, but Tommy now knew as much information as Azira on who this girl was and what she could do with computers, but more important, that she was willing to help.

"So, what have you found out about this operation?"

"Well, not much. It's run by some military big wig. I think she's being kept like a prisoner. She can't leave and she doesn't even know where it's located. Tommy, we've got to help her. We've got to get her out."

"Okay now, Azira, calm down. You've got to use your head on this and think this thing through. Now why would they let a bloody prisoner set up their computer security? Does that make sense?"

"It does if she thought she would be released if she cooperated. She's young and probably scared. She basically is being blackmailed. Forced into service and now she can't get away."

"Right, it's a possibility, I'll give you that; however, why go to those extremes when the government has tons of excellent computer people?"

"Maybe they didn't want anyone in the government to know what they were doing."

"But you just said it's being run by the military. That is the government. Or rather the military within the government."

"Tommy, you know as well as I do not all military factions control their governments and not all governments control their military factions."

Tommy was forced to agree on that one as well. "So, you think this is some secret, bastard military operation the government didn't sanction."

"I'm saying I don't know what's going on," Azira continued, "except there's a young girl who's scared, she's being kept against her will, and she's willing to help us find out what's going on. This has a lot more under the radar than hidden information on some cars and vans. If what you've told me so far is part of this, then conspiracy and murder are just the tip of their agenda."

"How soon can you contact this bird of yours again?" Tommy asked.

"I don't have real time contact yet. I can leave her a message. I don't know how soon she might check it. I'm sure she's watched. I can set up a program to let me know when she opens the site and see if it's safe for her to give me more details about the operation. Also, I might be able to track her down that way. But what do we do if she's in the Pentagon, or Cheyenne Mountain, or even Area 51?"

"There is no more Area 51, or at least that's what they say," Tommy said. "And if she's at some other big military complex, we'll, I don't know what we can do. We can't just go marching in and demand to see her, that's for bloody sure. The first thing we need to do is make regular contact with her and get as much information as we can. Information is the best weapon right now."

"I guess you're right," Azira said. "I'll get back to it and call you when I have more."

"I know I don't have to tell you, but mind yourself. Don't get yourself compromised. If these guys *are* the ones behind everything then they'll stop at nothing to keep their secrets."

"Don't worry. There's a saying among some computer black-hats; finding a secret is easier than keeping one."

"There's also a saying here in the FBI; when you're dead, you're dead."

Azira swallowed, "I think I like mine better."

Jenny was finishing her daily security updates for the operation on her computer before her shift was over. She set up additional firewalls on some sites and brought others up to date.

Her duties over the past couple months increased to include her checking personnel rosters to make sure everyone held the proper security clearances and they were issued the proper security badges for the sections they worked in. The security badges also doubled as the electronic entry badges for controlled access doors.

Unknown to any other computer techs working there, she secretly put in her own backdoor access codes. She gave herself access into all aspects of the operation now without anyone else being the wiser. It was easy. No one else there was as skilled.

She couldn't wait to get back into her secret site and see if there was a new message from *The Magician.* She was almost excited, but she needed to maintain her composure and not give any hint she was up to something. She needed to wait for the right moment.

She remembered playing *Evil Tempest* against him. Even then, she wondered what he was like. She never had a real boyfriend. She never made time. Most of her male contacts were at school or on line. At school, she was considered a nerd even though at that age it was evident she would turn out to be a beautiful woman. She didn't participate in sports, clubs, or social events and she was ignored by both the popular boys and girls of the *in* crowd.

On line, she was intimidating, overpowering. She was dominating over most games, including her own until she met a true challenge. Someone who could keep up. Match her at skill and speed and almost beat her.

Which was just before she was busted. She never got to talk one on one with the challenger. She just knew him as *The Magician.*

Now, here he was again. He found her. A magician, yes, but now her knight champion. She hoped his armor was shiny, and his sword swift and powerful. Powerful enough to conquer the evil general and rescue the young maiden. If only fairytales came true.

William N. Gilmore

CHAPTER 34

Sam was still holding his gun without pointing it at the big man and Debbie, having put hers away, took the tire iron into the kitchen and got Larry another cool cloth for his head. Larry, Sam, and Debbie were all sitting down at this point, waiting for Bubba the wrecker driver to open his mouth.

Bubba sat with his head down, not looking at anyone, breathing deeply.

"We're waiting on you," Larry began. "Do you have something to tell us or not? If nothing else, tell me why my head was used as the door knocker."

"It's a little embarrassing," he started out, just barely audible. "Do I have to tell you everything?"

There was a chorus of "yeses".

Looking up and giving a big sigh, Bubba began. "I was parked over off Armour Drive. There's never any traffic over there. Doris was with me."

"Who's Doris?" Debbie asked, not wanting to be left out now that she appeared to be part of the team.

"That's Sam's girlfriend."

Debbie turned her head quickly and looked at Sam. He thought she was about to pull her gun out again.

"Sam?" she slowly said, looking straight at him, eyes

285

squinting and taking in a deep breath.

"Sam Granger. The impound supervisor," Bubba said.

Debbie looked back at the wrecker driver and let the whole breath out at once, then looked back at Sam with a slight smile.

"Let's just keep calling him Granger if he comes up again," she suggested. "Much less confusing."

"Amen," Sam was heard to say under his breath.

Bubba nodded his head and continued, "We were parked over by an abandoned building in the dark. I saw a car, I couldn't tell what kind, being followed by the meat wagon and they pulled into a lot. The wagon pointed one way and the car the other like the drivers were going to talk.

The wagon started to pull off when I saw a flash and heard a pop. I thought it was a gunshot. The wagon kept going, but very slowly and it hit a tree and stopped.

"You and Doris saw Kim get shot?" Gillam exclaimed.

"Well, not Doris. Her head was in my lap, if you know what I mean." He looked over at Debbie, red faced, and said, "Excuse me, ma'am. That's what I didn't want to say." He sat there like a little boy waiting to see the principal.

Debbie looked down, a little red faced herself, trying not to laugh wondering how Doris managed any room to even get to that lap.

"Okay, that's all well and good, but continue with what you saw," Gillam said, a little frustrated. He still didn't know why he was holding a cool, wet rag to a bump the size of Stone Mountain on the back of his head.

"I saw the driver of the car get out and go over to the wagon and pull the guy out of the driver's seat and onto the ground. He searched him and the wagon, and then went around and pulled what looked like a body in a bag out of the back and put it in the trunk of his car. Was that a body?" Bubba asked.

"Yeah, I'm afraid so," Lovett answered in disgust, thinking about what happened to Kim. "Go on," he said, between clinched teeth.

"The guy looked all around. Doris was watching now. He didn't see us. He walked around the area for a few minutes, checked out the tree and picked up a long branch." Bubba held his arms out wide.

"Then he put the wagon driver back in the cab along with the branch and pushed him over so he could get in too. He backed the wagon up and drove down the street. The wagon turned around and stopped. The guy jumped out of the wagon, but the wagon kept going and was going pretty fast when it hit the curb. I thought it would hit the tree head on, but it just barely hit it and then the wagon flipped over several times and just sat there. The guy went up to it and looked around again."

"How well did you see this guy?" Gillam asked, hoping for the right answer.

"It was too dark then," Bubba said.

An even more frustrated Gillam told him to keep going.

"The guy went to the trunk of his car again and took out one of those big plastic gas cans. He went over to the wagon, took something out of the driver's side and poured gas all over it, inside and out, and then he set it on fire. It made a huge flame. I thought it would make the wagon explode. He put the can back in the trunk of his car and stood there, watching it for a short while. Like I said, the fire was huge. That's when I saw him. In the light of the fire. Then he got in his car and left."

Larry, Sam, and Debbie just looked at each other, mouths open. Debbie was the first to say anything.

"Oh, my God!" She said it for all of them.

"Bubba, are you saying you did see the guy who shot Kim, the driver of the wagon?" Gillam asked, trying to make sure what he heard was what was said.

"Yeah, I saw him. He was standing right there by his car when the flames were bright. He was smiling, too," he recalled with disgust. "Then he got out of there real fast. The fire department showed up just a few minutes later. Doris and I left while the firefighters were putting out the fire. I don't think nobody saw us."

"You didn't happen to see the license plate, did you?" Lovett asked, also hoping they would get lucky.

"No. We weren't that close. And it was at a bad angle."

"Too bad. I would love to run that plate.

"Are you going to kill me after I tell you all I know?" Looking at the big gun Lovett still held onto, he cowered back in the chair.

"Sam, put that thing away," Debbie admonished him. "He's trying to tell us what happened and you're over there scaring him. We're not going to hurt you, Bubba."

"No, we're just trying to find out who killed our friend, Kim," Sam said, holstering the gun."

"He was your *friend*? I thought you might be involved with killing him," he said, looking at Gillam. "I decided I was going to go tell Mr. Granger what I saw and if he'd help me, but then I saw you at the lot talking with him. I hid and didn't let nobody see me. Then I saw you were searching the wagon. It was just like what the other guy did."

"We were searching for evidence in the wagon," Sam said. "You said the other guy searched the wagon too?"

"No, I mean I saw him talking with Mr. Granger just like you guys did."

"I don't understand," Gillam said, looking confused.

"I thought you were involved with killing the guy because you were talking with Mr. Granger just like the other guy did. I thought I might be in trouble and needed to disappear."

"You're saying the guy who shot Kim was at the impound lot talking with Mr. Granger?" Gillam repeated the information. "When did he talk to Mr. Granger?"

"Right after I brought the wagon in that day. I dumped it and saw him at the office talking to Mr. Granger. I called Doris and told her to call, disguising her voice and ask for a wrecker for a car which wouldn't start at a false location so I could answer the dispatch call and head back out before Mr. Granger and the guy saw me. I was scared to go back. I thought for sure I would be dead."

"Okay. What makes you so sure that you were in any danger? You just picked up the wagon and dropped it off at the impound lot."

"I was scared someone seen me or the wrecker after all, or Doris said something and that's why he was talking to Mr. Granger. To find out who I was."

"That still makes no sense to me. Why would this guy be talking with Mr. Granger? What's that have to do with knocking me senseless with a tire iron?"

"The other guy got two goons working for him. They're bodyguards or something. I couldn't go against three or four. I got Doris to get your address for me, watched for you, and saw you were alone. I was going to make you tell me what you knew. Then I was going to call the FBI or CIA and have them come here and arrest you and then get the other guys."

"Okay, I get how you found me, but besides talking with Mr. Granger, what makes you think I work for this guy?"

"Because, you do."

"No, I don't."

"Yes, you do. He does too," nodding over at Sam.

"I don't think you know what you're talking about," Sam said.

"Yes, I do," insisted Bubba. "Doris and I know who it was."

The trio stared at Bubba as if he had two heads.

"You *know* who it was?" Gillam asked, more than surprised. "How do you know him, Bubba? Spit it out, tell us."

Bubba dropped the bombshell. "It was that lieutenant everybody hates. Your lieutenant. The one in charge of the Narcotics Squad."

To be continued in the
exciting new book

GOLD BADGES

&

DARK SOULS

A Larry Gillam and Sam Lovett Novel

by

William N. Gilmore

Coming Soon

Made in the
USA
Columbia, SC